W9-DCB-518

THE AUTOBIOGRAPHY OF MATTHEW SCUDDER

More by Lawrence Block

THE MATTHEW SCUDDER NOVELS

THE SINS OF THE FATHERS • TIME TO MURDER AND CREATE • IN THE MIDST OF DEATH • A STAB IN THE DARK • EIGHT MILLION WAYS TO DIE • WHEN THE SACRED GINMILL CLOSES • OUT ON THE CUTTING EDGE • A TICKET TO THE BONEYARD • A DANCE AT THE SLAUGHTERHOUSE • A WALK AMONG THE TOMBSTONES • THE DEVIL KNOWS YOU'RE DEAD • A LONG LINE OF DEAD MEN • EVEN THE WICKED • EVERYBODY DIES • HOPE TO DIE • ALL THE FLOWERS ARE DYING • A DROP OF THE HARD STUFF • THE NIGHT AND THE MUSIC • A TIME TO SCATTER STONES • THE AUTOBIOGRAPHY OF MATTHEW SCUDDER

THE BERNIE RHODENBARR MYSTERIES

BURGLARS CAN'T BE CHOOSERS • THE BURGLAR IN THE CLOSET • THE BURGLAR WHO LIKED TO QUOTE KIPLING • THE BURGLAR WHO STUDIED SPINOZA • THE BURGLAR WHO PAINTED LIKE MONDRIAN • THE BURGLAR WHO TRADED TED WILLIAMS • THE BURGLAR WHO THOUGHT HE WAS BOGART • THE BURGLAR IN THE LIBRARY • THE BURGLAR IN THE RYE • THE BURGLAR ON THE PROWL • THE BURGLAR WHO COUNTED THE SPOONS • THE BURGLAR IN SHORT ORDER • THE BURGLAR WHO MET FREDRIC BROWN

KELLER'S GREATEST HITS

HIT MAN • HIT LIST • HIT PARADE • HIT & RUN • HIT ME • KELLER'S FEDORA

THE ADVENTURES OF EVAN TANNER

THE THIEF WHO COULDN'T SLEEP • THE CANCELED CZECH • TANNER'S TWELVE SWINGERS • TWO FOR TANNER • TANNER'S TIGER • HERE COMES A HERO • ME TANNER, YOU JANE • TANNER ON ICE

THE AFFAIRS OF CHIP HARRISON

NO SCORE • CHIP HARRISON SCORES AGAIN • MAKE OUT WITH MURDER • THE TOPLESS TULIP CAPER

NOVELS

A DIET OF TREACLE • AFTER THE FIRST DEATH • ARIEL • BORDERLINE • BROADWAY CAN BE MURDER • CAMPUS TRAMP • CINDERELLA SIMS • COWARD'S KISS • DEAD GIRL BLUES • DEADLY

HONEYMOON • FOUR LIVES AT THE CROSSROADS • GETTING OFF • THE GIRL WITH THE DEEP BLUE EYES • THE GIRL WITH THE LONG GREEN HEART • GRIFTER'S GAME • KILLING CASTRO • LUCKY AT CARDS • NOT COMIN' HOME TO YOU • RANDOM WALK • RONALD RABBIT IS A DIRTY OLD MAN • SINNER MAN • SMALL TOWN • THE SPECIALISTS • SUCH MEN ARE DANGEROUS • THE TRIUMPH OF EVIL • YOU COULD CALL IT MURDER

COLLECTED SHORT STORIES
SOMETIMES THEY BITE • LIKE A LAMB TO SLAUGHTER • SOME DAYS YOU GET THE BEAR • ONE NIGHT STANDS AND LOST WEEKENDS • ENOUGH ROPE • CATCH AND RELEASE • DEFENDER OF THE INNOCENT • RESUME SPEED AND OTHER STORIES

NON-FICTION
STEP BY STEP • GENERALLY SPEAKING • THE CRIME OF OUR LIVES • HUNTING BUFFALO WITH BENT NAILS • AFTERTHOUGHTS 2.0 • A WRITER PREPARES

BOOKS FOR WRITERS
WRITING THE NOVEL FROM PLOT TO PRINT TO PIXEL • TELLING LIES FOR FUN & PROFIT • SPIDER, SPIN ME A WEB • WRITE FOR YOUR LIFE • THE LIAR'S BIBLE • THE LIAR'S COMPANION

WRITTEN FOR PERFORMANCE
TILT! (EPISODIC TELEVISION) • HOW FAR? (ONE-ACT PLAY) • MY BLUEBERRY NIGHTS (FILM)

ANTHOLOGIES EDITED
DEATH CRUISE • MASTER'S CHOICE • OPENING SHOTS • MASTER'S CHOICE 2 • SPEAKING OF LUST • OPENING SHOTS 2 • SPEAKING OF GREED • BLOOD ON THEIR HANDS • GANGSTERS, SWINDLERS, KILLERS, & THIEVES • MANHATTAN NOIR • MANHATTAN NOIR 2 • DARK CITY LIGHTS • IN SUNLIGHT OR IN SHADOW • ALIVE IN SHAPE AND COLOR • AT HOME IN THE DARK • FROM SEA TO STORMY SEA • THE DARKLING HALLS OF IVY • COLLECTIBLES • PLAYING GAMES

The Autobiography
of
Matthew Scudder

LAWRENCE BLOCK

The Autobiography of Matthew Scudder
Copyright © 2023, by Lawrence Block
All Rights Reserved.

ISBN: 978-1-954762-21-3

Author Photo by Amy Jo Block
Production by JW Manus

A LAWRENCE BLOCK PRODUCTION

MATTHEW SCUDDER

Introduction by Lawrence Block

Not for the first time, I've been invited to write about Matthew Scudder—not to produce another slightly fictionalized rendition of one of his cases, though I'm assured such would be welcome, but to furnish a biographical report on the man himself.

I can understand why I might be singled out for such a task. Scudder has been narrator and principal character in nineteen books of mine: seventeen novels, a collection of shorter fiction, and, most recently, a novella. I might be presumed to know something about him.

But the notion of writing about Scudder, of jotting down facts and observations about the fellow, has always rankled. I've turned surly when interviewers ask for a physical description, or seek out ways in which his personal history is or is not similar to mine.

An interviewer may wonder about Scudder's taste in music, or where he buys his clothes. Is he pro-choice? Does he vote? And some questions are oddly hypothetical. Has Scudder ever seen a UFO? What would he think if he did?

I turn away from those questions, even as I find myself wanting to turn away from this current assignment. Matthew Scudder has been a vital fictional presence in my life since I began writing about him in the final months of 1973. It's now the summer of 2022, and I'm at my keyboard with him very much on my mind.

And yes, that's very nearly half a century, and in all that time I can't recall ever having written about Matthew Scudder. I don't mean to be disingenuous here. The shelf holds nineteen books that might be said to constitute his ghostwritten autobiography, and it is not without reason that my name is on their spines and covers. I shaped them, I gave them dimension, I highlighted this and played down that. I feel comfortable calling them my books, and myself their author.

But don't ask me what he's like.

And yet the fellow who's assigned me this task is one whose friendship I cherish, and whom I find myself reluctant to disappoint. And perhaps there's a way for me to give him what he wants without overstepping the role I've played for all these years.

I'll do what I've always done. I'll step aside and let the man himself tell you as much or as little as he chooses.

Hard to know where to start.

With my birth, I suppose, and with the admission that my date of birth is not as you'll find it given in at least one of the books. They're factual renditions, or as factual as human memory and artistic requirements allow them to be, but sometimes they go a little astray. I don't know why Lawrence Block gave me a birthday in April or May, but he did, and went on to make the point that I was a Taurus, with the perseverance or stubbornness, as you prefer, that allegedly goes with that sun sign.

I can't deny the traits, but I am in fact a Virgo, born on September 7, 1938, in the Bronx Maternity Hospital on the Grand Concourse, the first child of Charles Lewis Scudder and Claudia Collins Scudder. I was named Matthew Collins Scudder, Collins because it was my mother's maiden name. As far as I know, there were no Matthews in the family. I think they just liked the sound of it.

We must have been living in the Bronx at the time, but we couldn't have stayed there very long, because we were in Richmond Hill when my brother was born at a hospital somewhere in Queens on December 4, 1941. They named him Joseph Jeremiah Scudder, and three days later the Japanese bombed Pearl Harbor, and two days after that my brother died, either from a congenital defect or complications of childbirth. I never knew exactly what happened, but I think the birth must have been problematic because it almost killed my mother. She was in the hospital until Christmas week. Her sister-in-law took care of me. That was my Aunt Peg, who was married to my mother's brother Walter.

I don't remember any of this. I remember knowing about it, because I was told, but I don't remember it. I had a brother for a little less than a week, and I never saw him.

"She was never the same after your brother's death." I heard that more than once from Aunt Peg, and from another aunt as well, probably Aunt Rosalie, although it could as easily have been Aunt Mary Katherine. I had a lot of aunts and uncles, most of them on my mother's side. My father had two sisters, Charlotte, who taught third grade and never married, and Helen, who was married and living in Kansas, I think Topeka, years before I was born. I met her once at my father's funeral. She flew in for the occasion, her first return to New York since she left, a bride fresh out of high school. I remember she homed in on me and told me childhood memories of my father, except she was drunk and they were the same two or three stories over and over.

They're all dead, of course, all the aunts and uncles. Helen had children, and at least one of them would have been older than I, because I believe it was her pregnancy that had propelled her into an early marriage, and out of New York. I never knew the names or even the number of her children, my first cousins, and have no idea if they're alive or dead.

And of course there were cousins on my mother's side, quite a few of them, but I've long since lost track of them. I could probably chase them down if I put my mind to it. There was a radio program when I was a boy, *Mr. Keen, Tracer of Lost Persons;* I don't know how keen I was, but I have had a fair amount of experience tracing people who were lost, and mostly wanted to stay that way.

These days Google makes it fairly easy. So far, though, I haven't made an effort in that direction, and I don't think I will. Elaine, my wife, swabbed her cheek and sent a Q-tip's worth of epithelial cells to Ancestry.com or one of its fellows, and she's learned a surprising amount about her ancestors on both sides, the Mardells and the Cheploves, along with being apprised periodically of some stranger bearing neither of those surnames with whom she shares a presumably significant amount of DNA.

I could send in a swab of my own. I know next to nothing about my grandparents and nothing at all of earlier generations of Scudders and Collinses—but what difference could it possibly make to know what heroes and scoundrels have nested in my family tree?

And, if I have a third or fourth cousin in Pembroke, Oregon, so what?

Or I might learn that Michael and Andrew, the sons of my first marriage, are not my only offspring. Half a century ago, both before and after my first marriage had run its course, I led an active sex life. I was drinking throughout those years, and I slept with strangers and allowed myself to assume they were on the Pill.

And what I now assume is that my partners in those adventures, who drank the way I did in the bars where I encountered them, weren't significantly more responsible than I. One of them could have carried a child of mine without knowing who'd fathered it.

Or without remembering me at all.

One hears stories. A letter, or more likely an email. "You don't know me, but I have reason to believe you might be my father . . ."

I think I'll leave my cheek unswabbed.

*   *   *

I doubt either of my parents was the same after my brother died. I'm just guessing, or perhaps inferring, because I have no memories of them before that unfortunate week.

They were good parents, I think. I was never spanked, let alone beaten, and if either of them ever raised a hand to the other I was not around to witness it. I don't remember many arguments, either, but when I try to recall those early years I have the sense of long silences, of afternoons and evenings when the only voice one heard was coming from the radio.

"There's good news tonight!"

That was Gabriel Heatter's tagline on his WOR news broadcast, and I can hear the words now in memory, in that rich and hearty voice. My father never missed Heatter's program, except when he failed to get home in time for it. I'm sure there must have been nights when the newsman didn't utter those words, because a world war was raging, and not every day of it included good news. But Gabriel Heatter apparently liked to see the bright side, and I think my father enjoyed those four words at least as much as he cared what had happened in the world.

Sometimes he'd come home late, long after the program, which my mother may or may not have troubled to turn on. "There's good news tonight!" he'd call out, echoing Heatter's cadence if not his vocal tone. And sometimes he'd leave it at that, or he might share the night's good news—a Yankees' victory, most likely. Like our forces in Europe and Asia, the Yankees were a rewarding team to root for. They won a good deal more often than they lost.

I don't know why I'm circling around this, so let me say it: He drank. On those nights when he missed Gabriel Heatter, he'd generally stayed longer than usual at whatever bar he favored at the time, but whenever he came home he smelled comfortingly of whiskey.

Comfortingly? A surprising word. Funny what a man hears himself say.

A comfort to Charlie Scudder, certainly, and I guess it was a comfort to me as well. That was his bouquet, his scent, and it meant Daddy was home.

He didn't stagger, didn't fall down. He might speak a little louder, but I don't recall his ever slurring his words. No personality change, no bursts of verbal or physical violence. He'd have something to eat, if he hadn't dined earlier, and he might get a bottle from the cupboard and pour himself a drink, and sip it while he smoked Chesterfields and listened to the radio or turned the pages of the evening paper.

He drank blended whiskey. The brands I recall all had numbers in them—Four Roses. Three Feathers. Seagram's Seven.

We moved often, it seems to me. We lived in the Bronx when I was born, and in Queens when my brother was born and died. We were still in Richmond Hill when I went to kindergarten, but halfway through first grade we moved, I think to Ridgewood or Glendale, and I had to go to a different school. It must have been a Catholic school, I remember nuns.

We weren't religious. My father's people were nominally Protestant, but nobody went to church. The Collinses were a mix of Catholic and Protestant, and I suppose if they'd been living in Belfast they'd have thrown bombs at one another, but nobody took it all that seriously.

My mother's sister Eileen was married to Norman Ross, who'd

changed his surname from Rosenberg. "Jews make good husbands"—I remember hearing one of my aunts make that declaration, and I never forgot it and wondered what it meant. I eventually worked out that it meant either that they were good with money or that they stayed away from the drink. Maybe both.

I don't know how Uncle Norman was with money, and I couldn't tell you if he drank heavily or moderately or not at all, but he didn't stay far enough away from the booze. He had a liquor store, and he got held up more than once, and the last person to point a gun at him pulled the trigger, and that was the end of Norman Ross, né Rosenberg.

A couple of years later Aunt Eileen remarried, again to a Jewish man. Uncle Mel's last name was Garfinkel, so I rather doubt he'd changed it, and he had a neighborhood hardware store on Queens Boulevard. Hardware stores get robbed less often than liquor stores, and as far as I know Aunt Eileen and Uncle Mel lived happily ever after.

Look, I'm an old man. My mind's like an old river, turning this way and that, and in no particular hurry to get where it's going. Meandering, that's the word for it.

* * *

My mother was always there, but there was always something tentative about her presence. She did all the things that she was supposed to do, she got up in the morning and fixed our breakfasts, she made beds and washed clothes and swept floors, she shopped for groceries, she put dinner on the table.

And she did all of this in near-silence. I don't think she had any friends outside the family. If the phone rang, and it didn't ring all that often, the caller would generally be one of her sisters with some sort of family news—somebody was sick or engaged or pregnant or dead.

If I was home I'd hear her end of the conversation. "Oh, that's too bad. Oh, how nice. Oh, I'm sorry to hear that."

She wasn't a drinker. She'd have a drink, at my father's urging, if there was something to celebrate, but she wouldn't have a second, and as often as not she'd leave her drink unfinished. And that reminds me of something I haven't thought of in years, how I found an abandoned drink of hers and polished it off. Just once, and I couldn't have been more than eight or nine years old, but even then I knew this was something I was not supposed to do.

But I wanted to, and no one was looking, and I drank it down. It must have been two ounces or so of what started life as whiskey and soda, but the bubbles were gone and it was mostly ice melt by the time I got my hands on it.

I liked the taste. I must have liked the idea of it, too. And the effect? I don't know that it had any, at least that I was aware of. And I both liked and disliked the fact that I had done something wrong. No one knew I'd done it, and nobody would ever find out (and I don't know that they'd have been all that upset if they did), but I was a good little boy, not much inclined to do what I wasn't supposed to do.

I remember making two decisions. First, that from now on if she abandoned a drink I'd leave it where it was, or pour it unsampled down the sink. Second, that whiskey was a Good Thing, and I'd drink my fill of it when I was old enough.

My fill and then some.

While she wasn't much of a drinker, my mother smoked, and I think she was a heavier smoker than he was. Whatever she was doing, she generally had a cigarette going. If she was cooking a meal or making a bed, there'd be a cigarette nearby, smoldering in an ashtray, waiting for her to reach for it. If she was sitting down and listening to the radio, there'd be a cigarette between her fingers, and after she'd crushed it out she'd soon enough light up another.

Like my father, she smoked Chesterfields. And of course my own first cigarettes were Chesterfields, taken surreptitiously from her pack. This would have been a few years after that first drink, and while I knew this too was a transgression, I don't recall being much bothered by the fact. What did bother me was the taste. One puff was as far as I got with that first cigarette, and while I would try others over the years, and smoke some of them halfway through, I never developed either a taste for tobacco or an addiction to it.

Not so for Claudia Scudder. I never saw her actually light one cigarette from the butt of another, but unless she was eating or sleeping she generally had a cigarette going. A carton couldn't have lasted her more than three days.

So three, four packs a day. When I was a boy a carton was two dollars, and a pack from a vending machine cost you a quarter. We never had much money, but even a heavy tobacco habit had minimal financial impact. Nobody ever had to give anything up in order to cover the cost of the next pack or the next carton.

I just checked now, I let Google save me a research trip to the corner deli, and the average cost of a pack of cigarettes in New

York City is $11.96. That's what, sixty cents a cigarette? They were a penny apiece when my mother smoked them.

Well, hell, they got her through the days, her cigarettes and her soap operas. On the radio for years, and then halfway through my second year in high school my father came home with a Philco television set, and before long she'd transferred her loyalties from mere voices and sound effects to characters she could actually see.

Progress.

It was the cigarettes that killed her, though they waited until just short of nine years after the drink killed him.

It's a slog, remembering all of this, writing it down. I think I'll take a break.

*   *   *

My father went from one job to another. I wasn't always aware of when one job ended and another began, and I didn't always know what it was that he did. For a while he drove a delivery truck for a bakery—I remember that because there were a couple of Saturdays when I rode along with him.

At one point he owned a shoe store. A neighborhood store, in the South Bronx. We were living somewhere else when he bought it—another part of the Bronx, or it could have been somewhere in Queens—and after he'd had the store for a month or two we moved to be closer to the store, and sometimes I would walk over there after school.

The shoe store failed before the year was out. We moved somewhere else. It's all gone now, the block the store was on, the block where we lived in the upper flat of a two-story frame house. All flattened in aid of the construction of the Cross-Bronx Expressway, and over the years I've never been on that stretch of highway without remembering the shoe store.

So the jobs never lasted too long, but neither did the periods of unemployment. He was, not to put too fine a point on it, a drunk, and drink has its effect on one's employment history whether or not one drinks during working hours.

I don't know what he may have thought about his drinking. He could have described himself, as I've heard quite a few people do, as a functioning alcoholic, and I understand the term, although I might change the modifier to *dysfunctioning*.

More often than not, I think he left jobs of his own volition. They were dead-end jobs, they were boring, they were too much work for too little money. And I'm sure there were times when the jobs left him.

He was an alcoholic and a depressive, although I never heard either of those words applied to him. He seemed to accept his condition—that his evenings would float on a river of whiskey, that nothing would ever quite work out for him, that the brief bloom of optimism that attended each change of occupation or residence would leave him back where he'd started, back where he'd always been.

I remember one night, largely indistinguishable from any other night. She was in the kitchen, he was in his chair in the living room with a glass in his hand. Three Feathers, Four Roses, whatever.

"Aw, Mattie," he said, and held the glass aloft, and looked at the ceiling light fixture through it. "This world's a hard old place. A man needs a little help to get through it."

*　　*　　*

I've told how he died. I'm pretty sure it wound up in one of the books, and maybe more than one, though like everything else in the books it may have been slightly shaped in the telling. The books are stories, and for all that their content is factual, they're deliberately fashioned as stories, each with a beginning and a middle and an ending.

I suppose human lives have those three things as well, though they're generally more clear-cut in books. Charlie Scudder's life was mostly middle, and I guess almost everybody's is, except for his second-born son, my brother Joe, who went in the blink of an eye from beginning to ending.

I hardly ever think about this brother I never saw and never knew. And now eighty years later it's as if he's right here in the room with me. Just at the boundary of my peripheral vision—which itself has been shrinking over the years.

Hovering, if you will, at the edge of thought.

Never mind. My father's own ending came one evening after he'd boarded the eastbound Canarsie Line subway at one or another of the stations on West Fourteenth Street. I don't know what had brought him into Manhattan that night, or what led him to take that particular Brooklyn-bound train.

I have to assume he'd been drinking. At that hour he'd surely have had a few, and maybe more than a few. And at some point he walked from one subway car to another, or at least walked from one car onto the passage between it and the next car. You weren't allowed to smoke on the subway, or anywhere in a subway station, but it wasn't unheard of for a straphanger to go out onto the platform between two cars and have a quick cigarette.

It was still illegal, of course. You were still smoking on the subway, even if you were no longer within one of its cars, and you were additionally in violation of a rule forbidding passengers from riding between the cars. Still, I never heard of anyone getting cited for it, or even cautioned.

Maybe the train stopped or started suddenly, or lurched. Or not. What difference does it make? He fell, and enough cars ran over him to mandate a closed casket.

There were more people at the funeral than I would have expected. Family, of course, but a lot of people I never saw before or since. Men, for the most part. I suppose they knew him from one job or another.

He was forty-three years old.

It was the end of August, the summer between my second and third years at Monroe. That's James Monroe High School, on Boynton Avenue in the Bronx. I probably shouldn't have gone there, I probably should have taken the test for Bronx Science, but that never occurred to me and no one ever suggested it.

Sometimes I think that tiny things that ought to be inconsequential have enormous consequences in life. Roads not taken, roads not even noticed in passing. Turn left instead of right, and a man who might have been CEO of General Motors winds up a second-shift barista at Starbucks.

And other times I think the opposite. He was always going to be a barista, no matter how many right turns he took along the way. He could go chase an MBA at Wharton, and he'd still wind up sculpting cute designs in the foam of your latte.

I lost a thread here. Where was I? Oh, right. At a funeral parlor on Gleason Avenue, looking at a closed casket.

And it was August, and I would turn seventeen in a few weeks. I had a job that summer, stocking shelves and delivering prescriptions for Perlstein's Pharmacy, but of course I had the day off.

Five or six days earlier, my father told me to call in sick. The Red Sox were in town, there was a game that afternoon at Yankee Stadium. "Tell the boss you're expecting a headache. And bring your glove. Maybe you'll catch a foul ball."

He must have taken me to, oh, ten or a dozen games over the years. Always Yankee games. New York still had three teams, the Dodgers and Giants wouldn't move west for another year or so, but I never got anywhere near Ebbets Field or the Polo Grounds. We might be living in Queens, but if we went to a ballpark, it was Yankee Stadium.

He was joking about the glove. There were kids, and even the occasional grown-up, who'd bring a baseball mitt to a game, on the off chance that somewhat might hit a foul ball in their vicinity. But we both thought such a move was impossibly lame, although I suppose we'd have used a different adjective back then.

I didn't bring a glove, nor did I call the drugstore. I said I wished I could but I really had to go to work, and he said oh well, another time. And then a few days later he took a cigarette break on the subway and that was the end of that.

"He was never the same after your brother died," she said. She spoke the words in an undertone while we waited for the service to begin, and expanded on them hours later, back home, after the last hangers-on had left.

He had always been a man of enthusiasms, she said. And that continued, and even after Joe's death, he'd greet a new job or a new business venture with a rush of energy and optimism.

But it wouldn't last. His mood would darken and his energy would sag, and the new enterprise would be an echo of all the ones that had preceded it.

"He was a good man, Matthew. He did the best he could. And he loved you."

*   *   *

Is anybody going to want to read all this?

I can't see why anyone would. But I seem to want to write it. I'm an old man, and there's something oddly bracing about a long look back at past years. Stir the pot and old memories bubble up. Most of them don't need to be written down, but the bit of attention I give them lights up the corners of long-abandoned rooms.

A woman writer—she was Southern, her name will come to me in a minute—said the bare fact of having survived childhood qualified her to be a writer. I suppose her point was that a person's early years provide an experiential base to draw from, for what it's worth. But what I took away from the remark was that childhood was something to be survived, and that every adult could take credit for that particular accomplishment.

My childhood was all right, and for all the time I now find myself spending on reexamining it, I've no need to share these reflections.

I'm not sure when my childhood ended. I don't know how one decides where to draw that line, or if there's an actual line to be drawn. Was I still a child up to the day my father died? In certain ways, perhaps, and not in others, and I'm not sure it's a question that needs to be asked, let alone answered, but one thing at least is clear. When he died, my childhood was over.

And I'd survived it.

* * *

If he'd lived, would I have gone to college?

That's hard to know. I was certainly bright enough for it, but my grades didn't always reflect my intelligence. I paid more attention in some classes than in others.

If I'd gone to Bronx Science, it would have been assumed that I'd go on to college. Nobody went there to prepare for a career as a longshoreman or a letter carrier.

But I'd gone instead to James Monroe, and some of my classmates went on to college and others did not. I don't know the numbers, but I wouldn't be surprised if they ran around fifty-fifty.

A coin toss.

I think my parents wanted me to go, or half-assumed I would do so. I remember my father musing that his life might have been a lot different if he'd gone to college, a prospect I don't think he'd ever entertained at the time.

My favorite subject in high school was Latin. I can't say what made me sign up for it my freshman year, and I remember my father rolling his eyes and observing wryly that it would come in handy when I entered the priesthood. I don't know why I liked Latin, but I did, and it was one subject I always got A's in. There was a kind of verbal logic to it that made perfect sense to me, and it improved my performance in English classes, too.

In second-year Latin we read Caesar's writing about the Gallic wars, and that same year in English we read *Julius Caesar*, Shakespeare's play, and the two went together nicely. I decided I liked Roman history, and looked forward to my junior year, when we'd be reading Cicero. And then a week or so before summer break, Miss Rudin asked me to see her after class.

I wondered what I'd done wrong. Nothing, as it turned out. I stayed after class, and so did a girl, Marcia Ippolito, and Miss Rudin was close to tears as she told us we two were the only students who'd signed on for third-year Latin, and that the school in its wisdom had elected to cancel the course.

Miss Rudin. I don't know how old she was at the time, old enough for gray hair, and probably thirty years older than I. Long gone by now, surely, but I never called her or thought of her as anything but Miss Rudin then, and apparently that hasn't changed.

Her first name was Eleanor. I'd forgotten that, but it came to me now, and it's the only thing I ever knew about her.

The woman who wrote about surviving childhood, her name was Flannery O'Connor. I knew it would come to me.

* * *

A couple of years ago I was in the Barnes & Noble near Lincoln Center—and it must have been more than a couple of years ago, because that store closed a while back. Elaine was looking for something to read, and I wandered around until my eye was drawn by a biography of Cicero by one Anthony Everitt. I bought it and read it, and it didn't make me go back and read Cicero, in Latin or in translation, but it was interesting enough to move me to pick up a nice three-volume edition of Gibbon's *Decline and Fall of the Roman Empire.*

I don't know that I'll ever make it past the first volume, but now and then I pick it up and read a few paragraphs or a few pages.

I can't see what difference it could have made if I'd been able to study a third year of Latin with Miss Rudin. Everything would have turned out the same. I'd have been a cop who'd read Cicero, and I'm not sure that would have been all that much of a distinction, not with all my brothers on the Force who'd gone to Catholic school.

Cicero or no, I wouldn't have gone to college. I don't think I'd have gone even if my father had stayed away from the Canarsie Line, I think I'd have been ready to be done with school, ready to get on with my life, whatever I might have thought that meant. But his death sealed things. I needed to bring money into the house. I needed to support myself, and my mother.

My first thought was that I'd drop out of school. I was within weeks of my seventeenth birthday, and I had my full height. I could get work.

I could have just found a job and failed to show up for school, but I announced my intention at the funeral, to an aunt or an uncle, and in no time at all I was given to understand that this was not what I was going to do. It was important, everyone agreed, that I get my high school diploma, and my mother echoed all of this and told me very firmly that I would complete my junior and senior years of high school and she didn't want to hear anything more about it.

I'd never heard her say anything so unequivocally. It left me feeling I ought to apologize for having so much as thought of dropping out, and it was clear that the matter was settled.

Meanwhile, there was a collection taken up, a metaphorical hat passed among the aunts and uncles. I wasn't aware of this while it was going on, but two or three days after the funeral Aunt Rosalie and Uncle Bert showed up at our apartment with an envelope. To tide us over, they said. They gave it to my mother, and I never did learn how much it contained. It was months later before I managed to ask, and the only answer I got was that people were very generous.

Uncle Bert told me that all I had to do for the next two years was get through high school, and that I should think about college. CCNY—that's the City College of New York—was right there in the Bronx, a long walk or a short bus ride away from where we were sitting, and was tuition-free, and a smart young man like myself should have no trouble getting in. "Just because they're mostly Jews there," he said, "doesn't mean it's an official requirement. You could go to classes and find work that fits your schedule. Just think about it."

I can't recall ever giving it much thought. I continued at James Monroe, and took a full schedule of courses, even if I didn't get to take Third-Year Latin. My junior year I stayed on at Perlstein's, stocking shelves and delivering prescriptions from 3:30 until the store closed at 7:00.

I had different jobs on Saturdays. Only one of them was interesting, and it only lasted a little over a month. It was for some sort of market research firm, and it involved going door to door in the Parkchester section of the Bronx and asking people how they felt about instant coffee. I carried a clipboard and a ballpoint pen, and I asked the questions on the sheet they'd given me and noted the responses.

You had to wear a short-sleeved white dress shirt and a tie. I guess it was supposed to make you look serious or respectable or both.

What made the job interesting wasn't the shirt and tie, or what anybody had to say about instant coffee. What was interesting was that I never had the slightest idea what would be on the other side of the door I was knocking on. Half the time nobody was home, and a number of those who were found some way to tell me to fuck off, but a lot of doors opened for me and I got to look at a lot of people's lives, however briefly.

And, you know, it had a lasting effect. Early on, I had to force myself to knock on each of those doors. I don't know that I was scared, but at the very least I was apprehensive. It wasn't as challenging as door-to-door sales, I wasn't asking anybody to buy anything, but there was an unwelcome element of confrontation involved.

But I did it, and the more I did it the less it bothered me, which I guess is the way that sort of thing works. And some years later I remember an instructor at the Police Academy telling us all that the acronym GOYAKOD embodied the most essential basic element of police work. And what did it stand for? Get Off Your Ass and Knock On Doors.

And I already knew how to do that.

Oh, here's an odd thing. There was a classmate of mine at Monroe who had the same job, white shirt and tie, clipboard, knocking on doors. His name was Eddie Towns, and I hadn't really known him until we both landed the instant coffee gig. I noticed that his shift took him half the time I was spending, and we compared notes, and he was surprised to learn that I was actually knocking on all those doors and talking to the people who opened them.

And I was at least as astonished to discover that he wasn't. He'd knock on a few doors and go through a few interviews, but what he mostly did was make up his own answers to the questionnaire. "Because who gives a shit, right? You think anybody even looks at what we turn in? You think some genius on Madison Avenue changes an ad campaign because Mrs. Kelly at 537 Jerome Avenue thinks Yuban instant coffee smells like dirty socks?"

Either Eddie or I was being stupid, and I kept changing my mind as to who it was. I figured he'd get fired, and he might have, sooner or later, but the instant coffee study ran its course and when it was over they let us both go. He did things his way and I did things mine, and I guess we both came out okay.

Was it morality or fear of the consequences that kept me on the straight and narrow? Looking back, I think the chief factor may have been inertia. And what would I do with the hour or two that I saved?

And virtue, it turned out, had unanticipated rewards. One Saturday afternoon I knocked on a door on Glebe Avenue and the woman who opened her door for me went on to offer me a cup of coffee. (That wasn't unusual, given the subject of my questionnaire.) As usual I declined, I wouldn't develop a taste for coffee for another couple of years, so she suggested a Coke or a beer. I said yes to the beer, and she contrived to bump into me on her way to the kitchen, and again on the way back, and you can see where this is going. I couldn't, not at first, but I caught on soon enough, and it took me longer than usual to finish that day's shift.

Her name was Shirley Rasmussen, and she said she was thirty-five, which seemed very old to me. Looking back, I think she was probably closer to forty. She was married, and if she ever told me her husband's name I've long since forgotten it. He was out for the afternoon, he'd taken both their kids to the Knicks game and hadn't even asked her to come along, not that she would have. Basketball wasn't her game.

We played her game in their bedroom, with a crucifix on one wall and the Sacred Heart of Jesus on another. If I'd been Catholic that might have given me pause, but probably not; all I knew was I was actually going to get laid, and I didn't have room in my mind for anything else.

I suppose nowadays people would label her behavior as child molestation. I was seventeen, a young seventeen, and she was more than twice my age. A lot of people would contend that she took advantage of me.

And, you know, if you were to reverse the genders, if you

make Shirley a forty-year-old man having his way with a seventeen-year-old girl, I'd join in that judgment. I know that's inconsistent, that sauce for a goose is equally sauce for a gander, but it seems categorically different to me.

I saw her four more times after that, spread over two months or so. Always around one o'clock on a weekday afternoon, while her husband was at work and before her kids got out of school. I'd invent a medical appointment and leave school early.

She wasn't beautiful, and I suppose both her face and figure were past their prime, but she was still an attractive woman, and her sexual energy and enthusiasm were a big part of the draw. I don't suppose she was sexually more knowledgeable than most women of her age and in her circumstances, but if you'd shown me a copy of the *Kama Sutra* I'd have assumed she wrote it. She knew what she liked and she knew what she wanted and she wasn't shy about letting me know.

Just that first Saturday, and then four weekday afternoons. On the last of these she said we'd had a lot of fun, but now it was time to stop. "Before either of us likes the other too much," she said. I said something awkward, maybe that I already liked her a whole lot, and she said that was all the more reason to call it quits. But first there was one more thing we'd never tried . . .

Afterward, on my way home, I felt the disappointment one would expect, but I was surprised to find I also felt a measure of relief. It was the sort of thing that had to end, and it might very easily have ended badly in any number of ways, and instead it had come to a very satisfactory conclusion, leaving me with new knowledge and experience and nothing but pleasant memories.

And by the time I got home I found myself thinking about one of the girls in my English class. It took me a few days to work up the courage, but I pictured myself in front of a door with her name on it, and I went ahead and knocked. Would she like to go to a movie? Sure, she said.

*   *   *

Did I ever tell anybody about Shirley? Only Elaine, and that was years and years later, when the two of us were treating each other to guided tours of Memory Lane. Aside from that, I don't believe I ever told a soul.

It was the kind of thing high school boys boast about to their friends, but I didn't have the kind of friendships that called for that sort of conversation. And I'm not sure why, but it felt like something I ought to keep to myself.

It came to mind a couple of years ago, when that high school teacher in Maine was caught having an affair with one of her fifteen-year-old students. She got prison time for it, remarkably enough, and actually served a couple of years, and got headlines upon her release by marrying the boy.

We were talking about it with Mick and Kristin Ballou, and all agreed it was a hell of a story, storybook ending and all, and the prison sentence was the most astonishing element of it.

"You don't put a woman like that in jail," Mick said. "You give her the fucking Medal of Honor."

*   *   *

I worked non-union construction the summer between my junior and senior years. We did repairs and remodeling for landlords, and then our crew got a big job, working on a three-story frame house in Kingsbridge. It had been chopped up into a real rabbit warren, and we ripped out partitions and turned it back into a duplex, and brightened up the exterior with aluminum siding.

I wasn't particularly handy, but if you showed me how to do something I could generally get the hang of it, and nobody expected us to work ourselves to death. I got along with everybody, and the pay was good, $2.50 an hour, more than twice what I'd made at Perlstein's. And I got paid in cash, with no taxes deducted.

Come September, the house in Kingsbridge was still a long way from done, and they'd have been happy to have me stay. That would have been fine with me, too, but my mother wouldn't hear of it, and a guy in my crew steered me to a pair of brothers from some part of what was still Yugoslavia. They painted apartments, slapdash work for landlords, and they needed somebody on weekends. Only two dollars an hour, and it was good they never had much to say because I couldn't get past their accents, but the work wasn't too bad.

So that was how I spent my Saturdays, and about half my Sundays. Another kid had replaced me at Perlstein's, but there were plenty of drugstores in the Bronx, and I found one that could use me from when school let out until they closed at seven.

I went to my classes, but I can't say they got much of my attention. That was senior year, so the Shakespeare play we studied in English Four was *Hamlet,* but the experience didn't make much of an impression.

We saw *Julius Caesar* on TV a couple of years ago and there were speeches I could have recited along with the actors. We watched *Hamlet* a year later and, except for the lines everybody knows, it was all new to me. And that would seem to say more about my time at James Monroe than it says about the plays.

*   *   *

In the books, some of my experiences have been shaped into vehicles for entertainment. Each is about a case of one sort or another, and there's an investigation, and eventually a resolution. They're novels, they have a shape to them. Each one tells a story.

And what the hell am I writing now? I suppose it's the part between the books, the part you'd skip. And why shouldn't you? I mean, who cares?

Elaine might. She'll read these lines with interest. We've pretty much told each other everything—and more than once, as like as not—but it seems to me there are things here I've never troubled to mention.

More to the point, it's interesting to me. One reaches an age when the past is as interesting as the present, and a bit less difficult to make sense of.

So I'll go on. You don't have to. Your call.

*   *   *

Graduation was different things to different people. For those who'd be going on to college, it was a way station; for those of us who weren't, it was a much bigger deal, a specific moment when a kid became a grown-up.

There were parties following the ceremony, parties where parents poured drinks for their kids' classmates. (And in most cases without breaking the law. The drinking age in New York was still eighteen, and most of us had already reached that mark.) I went from party to party, and woke the next morning with no recollection of having left the last party and no idea how I got home. Did I walk? I didn't drive, having neither a car nor a license, but did someone give me a ride?

I'd had my first blackout, although I didn't know to call it that. I did know that this sort of thing happened if a person drank too much, which I'd evidently done.

No harm. I woke up in my own bed with no symptoms beyond a thirst it took a whole quart of water to quench.

I've told this story at AA meetings. No need to drag it out now.

*   *   *

What I was getting at—at the graduation parties, there was something I heard more than one or two of my classmates say. "From here on in it's all downhill."

Like this was the high point of the lives they were destined to lead. The glory years of high school were behind them, and all the future could be expected to hold was a dead-end job, pushing papers or a hand truck.

That's if you were a boy. If you were a girl you'd spend the rest of your life making beds and washing clothes and cooking meals and wiping kids' noses and bottoms. Or maybe you'd wind up emptying bedpans at a hospital or teaching geography to fifth-graders who didn't care about any place you couldn't get to on the D train.

All downhill.

I may have echoed the sentiment, or at least nodded along with it, but I didn't really see it that way. I couldn't picture my time at James Monroe as any sort of glory years, and in a sense I'd had an early graduation when my father took that cigarette break on the Canarsie line.

And something else. I had two jobs lined up, one in a construction crew not unlike where I'd worked the previous summer, the other an evening shift in the warehouse at a freight-handling company. They were both dead-end jobs, but I didn't expect to be working either of them for the rest of my life.

I don't know that I could have told you this at the time, but I never ceased to be essentially optimistic at heart. The future was invisible, out of sight beyond the horizon, but an invisible future could as easily turn out to be bright as dark.

Did I get this from my father? The world, he'd assured me, was a hard old place, and there's no question he saw a dark side to it.

But there was something that made him pick himself up whenever he fell down, something that always steered him to a new job after he'd walked away from an old one. Maybe it was the same thing that led him to reach for the drink that might give him a lift.

However I came by it, somewhere within myself I knew that the life I was leading was temporary. I'd get through it, and there'd be something interesting on the other side.

First, though, I had to wait for my mother to die.

*　　*　　*

Not consciously.

I worked my two jobs, painting and patching plaster mornings and afternoons with Harry Ziegler's crew, shifting parcels and crates evenings at Railway Express. I lived at home, of course. Where else would I live?

She was almost always up in time to make my breakfast. I'd started drinking coffee by then, and she'd pour me a cup and put something in front of me, a couple of eggs or some cereal. It was Hobson's Choice and she was Hobson, and that was fine because I didn't really care whether I had two over easy or a bowl of Grape-Nuts.

She'd sit across the table from me, and drink a cup of coffee. And smoke a Chesterfield or two.

At first I would generally make it home for dinner, but I didn't have all that much time between my day and evening jobs, and sometimes there was a change of trains involved in getting from one to the other. It was easier to pick up something along the way, a slice of pizza or a deli sandwich, and then I discovered the steam table at a Blarney Stone around the corner from Railway Express. They'd never get any Michelin stars, but the food was tasty enough, and the price was right, and instead of a snack you were getting a balanced meal.

And you could improve the balance with a glass of beer.

Or even two. I wondered if anybody at Railway Express would care, until I realized that most of my co-workers were half in the bag themselves. The manager kept a bottle of Old Crow in his desk, and I never heard him say anything about his drinking, or anyone else's.

I might have a drink afterward, on my way home, or I might not. I'd almost always find her in the kitchen, smoking a cigarette, looking at something on the television set. I'd sit a while and we'd talk, and you'd think I could remember what we talked about, but all those conversations just drifted away like plumes of smoke.

Smoke.

She would cough. It was what even in those relatively innocent times everybody called a cigarette cough. It got worse over time, as everything always does, and sometimes she'd be wracked with coughing and unable to stop. And then she'd get hold of herself, and say *These damn things!* and crush out the current cigarette, and a few minutes later she'd light the next one.

Why drag this out? I guess she must have had COPD for years, although it would be many more years before I ever heard the term. When she finally saw a doctor he told her it was emphysema, and it couldn't be reversed, but if she stopped smoking it could be arrested, or at least slowed down.

She tried to stop, and couldn't, and the next time she went to the doctor he took an x-ray and diagnosed lung cancer, although I don't believe she ever spoke the word.

"He took an x-ray. He found, you know, what you'd expect to find."

Mustn't say the C-word. You could die of it, but don't ever fucking say it out loud.

Nowadays there'd be radiation and chemo, and she might get years out of it, maybe even enough of them to wind up dying of something else. And if she'd had Blue Cross, or pots of money, perhaps they'd have tried something that I'm sure she was better off without.

I found a woman in the building who'd be with her days, and I quit my job at Railway Express, and I'd pick up a six-pack on my way home and drink a beer or two in front of the TV. I wasn't well cast as Florence Nightingale, but you do what you have to do, and I didn't have to do it for very long.

I've heard it said that everybody stops smoking, that the trick is to be alive when it happens. She stopped shortly after the x-ray, but not for lack of trying; she just couldn't smoke anymore, she'd start coughing before she could inhale the first lungful.

So she was alive when she stopped, but the craving persisted for five months, until the night her heart gave out. I looked in on her in the morning, and she was gone.

* * *

Jesus, this is all about death, isn't it? This one dies and that one dies and life goes on until it doesn't.

* * *

I went back and read what I'd written, and tried to think what to write about next, and then Elaine mentioned something she'd read about online, an old railroad line with a steam engine operating out of Utica, New York. You took an Amtrak train to Utica, four hours away, and after your excursion on the old train you had an interesting choice of restaurants and accommodations and things to look at.

And so we took a three-day break, which was just the right amount of time for Utica, and two days after we got back we had Mick and Kristin Ballou over for dinner. Elaine made pasta and a salad, which is essentially her default meal, and nobody drank anything stronger than decaf.

A mutual acquaintance had died in our absence, and we speculated as to when and where the funeral might be—it hadn't been announced yet, and might well be across the river in Jersey—and whether any of us felt obliged to go. I don't know that we reached a conclusion, but someone remembered an observation that gets attributed, probably apocryphally, to Yogi Berra: *"If you don't go to other people's funerals, how can you expect them to come to yours?"*

"Ah, Jaysus," Mick said. "Matthew, will I go to yours or will you come to mine?"

The question just hung in the air, and then he said, "A terrible thought either way, so maybe we'll be like McGuinness and McCarty."

Blank stares.

"You don't know the song?"

Nobody did.

He sang, to a tune I suppose was an Irish jig or reel:

> *"Oh, McGuinness is dead and McCarty don't know it,*
> *McCarty is dead and McGuinness don't know it,*
> *They're both of them dead in the very same bed—*
> *And neither one knows that the other one's dead."*

That changed the subject, and not a moment too soon. It reminded Kristin, I'm not sure how, of a song that was neither morbid nor Irish but recounted the elaborate set of marital circumstances that led to a young man's marriage to a woman who was technically his grandmother. *I'm My Own Grandpaw* was the title everybody remembered, but no one could manage to recall how the song went.

I could Google my way to the lyrics. I could probably listen to the song on YouTube. But why would I want to?

*　　*　　*

Before the evening ended, we spoke more of death. Some remark put me in mind of Danny Boy and the list he'd made of everyone he knew who had died. He'd kept it up for quite a while, until whatever had led him to begin had run its course, and he could find another area to be compulsive about.

"Danny Boy Bell," Mick said. "There's one I'd have to call African-American, because it's too much of a stretch to call him black. An albino, I guess he is, and white as a bedsheet."

Elaine said that was why black was capitalized these days, to show that it wasn't about color, and Kristin said but it was about color, and Elaine agreed that everything was about color. That stopped the conversation, until Mick brought it back to Danny Boy and asked if both his parents had been black. Or Black, as you prefer.

I said that was what I understood, although I'd never met either of them, and then I remembered something Danny Boy had told me the last time we'd spoken. "He hired a genealogist," I said, "and traced his ancestry back to the royal family of the Kingdom of Dahomey."

"Is that a fact?" Mick said, and I said Danny Boy thought it was, and promised next time he'd show me a copy of the family tree the woman had drawn up for him. He didn't say what he'd paid her, but clearly felt it was money well spent.

"The prince," Elaine said, "formerly known as Danny Boy." She'd known him almost as long as I had, and she'd been sitting at his table the night I first saw her. "How is he, Matt?"

He'd had health problems, but I don't know many people who haven't. But it has been a while, probably a few years, since I'd seen him. His eyes and his skin made sunlight an enemy, and all his life he'd kept vampire's hours; nowadays I myself was increasingly early to bed and early to rise, though I can't say the effects were as the adage promised.

"I suppose he's all right," I said. "Otherwise I think I'd have heard. If he died, wouldn't somebody have called me?"

"Ah," Mick said. "Unless the person who'd have called you was dead his own self, and here we are again with McCarty and McGuinness."

"In the very same bed," Kristin said. "Elaine, I guess this is what you and I get for marrying a couple of old men. I was hoping for wisdom, and all I get is McGuinness and McCarty."

*   *   *

Age is probably a part of it. The past keeps gaining ground on the future, and part of living is outliving others, and nothing this side of dementia can keep you entirely unaware of the process. Life, even as it lengthens, becomes increasingly about death.

And yet it seems to me that my life has always been about

death. During those years when I carried an NYPD badge, it was matters of life and death that got my full attention.

The job changed my view of the world. It generally does, from the day you first put on the blue uniform. A few years ago I heard someone use the term *moral relativism*, and I was interested enough to look it up. There's a character in a French play who's gobsmacked to learn that what he's been speaking his whole life is called prose, and if I wasn't quite as startled by what I read, I had much the same moment of recognition.

A moral relativist? *Moi?*

And there's something wrong with that?

I don't know that cops all grow into moral relativists, and in fact I've known more than a few with a hard and fast, take-no-prisoners view of right and wrong. But many of us watch the moral world go in and out of focus, and learn that not all crime cries out for punishment, and not all rules need to be enforced, and that what's right and what's wrong depends on who you are and where you've planted your feet.

Except for murder.

Because, as I saw it, as I guess I've always seen it, taking a life is different. The only cases I really cared about were homicide cases. The conventional wisdom is nonsense, people do get away with murder, and it never ceased to bother me.

Other crimes were part of the ebb and flow of urban life—and rural life too, I suppose. There were crimes without victims, prostitution and gambling and serving alcohol after hours, and they offered profit possibilities for the police officer who looked the other way. And there were endless nonviolent varieties of larceny and fraud, and how much they concerned you depend-ed upon the strength of your commitment to law and order.

And so on.

But murder was something else. Taking a life was categorically different from taking a liberty or taking a wallet.

That principle, if I can call it that, has always been part of who I am. The ways in which I see the world and my role in it are apt to change from day to day. Ages ago a waitress at Jimmy Armstrong's asked my date of birth and told me I was a Virgo, which was hardly news to me, and that mine was one of the four mutable signs. And what did that mean? That I was changeable and adaptable and flexible, she explained, and ready for something new. As apparently was she.

I can't remember her name. It'll come to me.

Never mind. I see many things differently from time to time, little things like politics and religion—and, come to think of it, astrology.

But, you know, the mutability stops when the man with the broad ax steps onto the stage. The phrase and image are Mick's, it's how he pictures Death, his take I suppose on the Grim Reaper and his scythe.

If he's not onstage, he's in the wings, waiting for his cue. The bastard's never very far away.

Well, I suppose I come by the preoccupation honestly. I was in my teens when I lost my father and not far into my twenties when my mother followed him.

And even before that.

In seats at Sunnyside Gardens, between rounds: "*Your mother's never been the same after your brother died.*"

At Gleason's, side by side in front of a closed casket: "*After we lost your baby brother, he was never the same man.*"

And what of young Matthew? I'd never laid eyes on Joseph Jeremiah Scudder, was never in the same room with him, or even the same building. He came and went in a matter of days, and I've no memory of any of it.

But I must have been aware, don't you think? Back then, while it was going on. I was three years old, for God's sake, and presumably conscious and sentient during my waking hours. I was, as I said, at Aunt Peg's while they were in hospital, and she and Walter would surely have talked about what was going on, if in hushed tones. I'd have been told early on that I had a baby brother, and wasn't that wonderful, and then when it ceased to be wonderful there'd have been tears and lamentations, and I'd have picked up on it.

There was a period of time when they weren't sure my mother would live, when it seems very possible that she'd follow her baby boy to the grave. How could you keep something like that from a three-year-old? For Christ's sake, you couldn't keep it from a house plant.

Of course I'd have known. What I'd have made of it, what I might have thought about it, well, who's to say? But I'd have to have known, however quickly it may have vanished from the Magic Slate of memory.

"*Little Matt was never the same after his baby brother died.*"

Nobody ever said that, and I don't know that it's true. But, you know, it's not out of the question.

*   *   *

After I'd buried my mother, one of the first things I did was go back to Railway Express. The boss there was apologetic; they'd replaced me, but as soon as they had an opening it was mine. He had my number, but it might be a good idea to check back with him from time to time.

He never called, and neither did I, because it dawned on me that I didn't need to work two jobs with only myself to support. And I could give our flat back to the landlord and find myself a smaller apartment.

No hurry there. The rent was reasonable, and if the apartment still held a sickroom vibe, it also retained the virtue of familiarity. I knew the neighborhood, the bars and coffee shops, where to drop off my laundry, where to pick up a newspaper. Move more than a couple of blocks and you had to learn those things all over again.

Speaking of learning, Harry Ziegler thought I should learn a trade. He ran a non-union crew, but he held cards himself in two craft guilds, plumbers and plasterers, and if the crew fell apart or the jobs stopped coming, he could hire on somewhere and draw union pay until it was time to start collecting a union pension.

Plastering was a beautiful trade, he told me, and you wouldn't want to meet a nicer guy than your average plasterer, but when was the last time anybody used lath and plaster in new construction? It was all sheetrock now, and you'd still run into signs urging you to Keep New York Plastered, but it was a lost cause.

"But there's gonna be jobs for plumbers, Matt, as long as you and I and everybody else find the time for a shave and a shower and so on. Until they invent something to take the place of water, you're gonna need people to make it go in one direction and not in the other. You're a plumber, your phone might ring in the middle of the night, which your plasterer doesn't have to contend with, and when the day's done you'll spend a lot of time washing your hands, but once you're a union plumber you'll never miss a meal. Unless" —patting his stomach— "unless you got a wife puts you on a diet."

I can't say I was caught up in the romance of plumbing, in or out of a union. But what he'd said made good sense. I had a strong back and a high school diploma, neither of which qualified me for anything in particular. Harry thought he could find somebody to take me on as an apprentice, and when I got to the end of that road I'd be employable for the rest of my life.

It was the path of least resistance, and I could have found myself on it, even as I found myself staying on in the house where my mother had died.

And if I had? Who knows where it might have led, or what kind of life I'd have lived. One sure thing, I'd have thought, is that I wouldn't find myself writing about it, but I just Googled "memoirs of a plumber" and learned that there were more people than I'd have guessed who'd traded a pipe wrench for a keyboard.

Never mind. My mother died, and six months later I sat in a roomful of men on East Twentieth Street and took the NYPD's police officer entrance exam. I expected to pass, and I did, and a month later I reported to the same building and started my training.

That may have been destined, if there's such a thing as destiny. But maybe not. Family connections mean more on the other side of the law, but a lot of cops are the sons of cops, and there were no law enforcement officers on either side of my family. (Or criminals either, to my knowledge.)

It's my guess that anybody's destiny works better when it gets a helping hand. Mine got a boost at my father's funeral.

*   *   *

The family was there, of course, with everybody saying pretty much the same thing. Such a young man, and wasn't it a shock, and you never know, do you. And what a good man to have such a hard life come to such an early end.

And so on. The things you'd expect, and the people who weren't relatives, most of them people I didn't know, said much the same thing. A few of them told me who they were, and so I knew they'd worked alongside him, or swapped stories with him on adjacent barstools.

"Your dad was proud of you."

I heard that a lot, but it came across as part of the soundtrack. *Guy's dead, managed to get himself underneath a subway car, here's his kid, what are you gonna say to him? "Your dad was real proud of you."*

Somewhere in the course of things, a man around my father's age approached me on his own and told me his name was Stan Gorski. He was wearing a dark suit, I remember, which wasn't unusual in that crowd, but it was warm at Gleason's, and most of the men had taken off their ties, or at least loosened them.

He hadn't. He said, "You're Matt, and we haven't met, but I saw you with your dad a little over a year ago. At Saint Nick's."

St. Nicholas Arena, in the West Sixties. And gone in the early Sixties, but for the preceding half century they had boxing matches there. My dad and I only went there the once. The few other fight cards we saw were at Queens, at Sunnyside Gardens.

"I was working," he said, "or I'd have come over and said hello. I didn't know Charlie all that well but I liked him."

I remembered the names of the fighters in the main event, and seized upon that as something to talk about. Stan asked me if boxing was my favorite sport. I said I liked it, and I liked baseball and football, but not to play. I wasn't very good at sports, I said.

Had I ever done any boxing?

Uh, no.

I remember he looked me up and down, which I've always thought of as an expression, but he did just that, looked me up and down. He said I might like it, and talked about the Police Athletic League, and how it was all free of charge, and the training was a great way to get in shape.

We talked for a while. A lot of people spoke to me that day, but this was the only real conversation.

He gave me a slip of paper with his name and phone number on it, and I thought I might call, but of course I didn't. And then one night my mother answered the phone and it was for me, which it never was, and it was Stan Gorski. He started to remind me who he was, but of course I remembered him and the conversation we'd had.

I guess he caught me at just the right time. A day or two later I found my way to the parochial school gym where Stan put in ten or a dozen volunteer hours a week teaching high school kids how to jump rope and hit a heavy bag.

It turned out he was right. I liked it.

There were kids I only saw there once, and others for whom it was a daily event. I got there once or twice a week, and told myself I'd go more often, but never seemed to. Jumping rope was probably good for me physically, but I can't say I liked it much. Working the speed bag was tricky at first, I think it is for everyone, but I got a little better with practice.

But what I liked was the heavy bag. I'd wrap the cloth tape around my hands and slip on a pair of red Everlast gloves and get to business. I learned how to punch, how to get my jab out there, how to throw a hook or a straight right.

"No arm punches, Matt. Punch from the shoulder, and put your whole body into it."

I learned how to do that. The heavy bag had nothing to worry about, it could take more than I could throw at it, and it wasn't even breathing hard when my hands dropped and I knew I was done for the day. It was exhausting, slugging away like that, but my body responded to it, and not just the arms and chest and shoulders. I firmed up on the midsection—nobody called it the core then—and the lower body as well.

And I don't know how aware of it I was at the time, but I think it did something for the way I felt about myself and the world around me. My father was gone, and his legacy to me was a mix of obligations and diminished expectations, and I don't know how much that weighed on me, but what I do know is I always felt better after a session with the heavy bag.

Some days, if there was time, Stan would slip on a pair of mitts and catch the punches I threw at them. I enjoyed that. And sometimes he'd have two us pair off and do a little light sparring. We'd have mouthpieces and protective head gear, and nobody I ever saw at St. Margaret's would remind you of Jack Dempsey, or showed much in the way of killer instinct.

But I can't say I liked it much. I didn't care for getting hit, I felt clumsy throwing punches that didn't find their target, and I remember landing a body punch and having the sense of accomplishment entirely erased when I saw my opponent wince. I hadn't hit him that hard, I saved what power I had for the heavy bag, but I got him in the solar plexus, and I guess he felt it.

There was one boy, a welterweight, who showed promise, and Stan steered him to a credentialed gym where he could get on track for the Golden Gloves. The rest of us were getting a good workout and developing some basic skills, and the year's highlight would be a card of eight or ten matches with a similar PAL group who trained at the Elks Club in Woodside.

I'd have been expected to take part, but it was after the school year ended, and I quit showing up at St. Margaret's and worked construction full-time. I told Stan I'd see him in the fall, and maybe I meant it, but it didn't happen.

*　　*　　*

"Write something every day. Sit down at your desk, first thing in the morning's the best time, and just write a sentence and see where it leads you.

"And don't go back and read what you've done. Just keep going forward. When you're all done, that'll be time enough to have a look at it."

*   *   *

My instructions, and I could see the point.

Yesterday morning I poured myself a cup of coffee and sat here at my desk. I looked at the screen for a while, wrote a sentence and deleted it, wrote another sentence and changed a couple of words around before deleting it.

I remembered typing up my reports, as a patrolman and later as a detective. The only way to change a sentence around was to put a fresh sheet of paper in the typewriter and start over. It's a lot easier now.

I never wrote a sentence yesterday that I didn't delete, and I didn't try more than two or three times over ten or twenty minutes. Then I scrolled up to the top of the document and read *"Hard to know where to start,"* which struck me as true enough if not particularly eloquent. And I read on from there.

Which I'd been advised not to do, but I have a mixed record when it comes to doing what I'm told.

I read it all the way through. When I'd finished I thought about deleting all those words, or dragging the whole file into the Trash. The impulse was definitely present, but I guess I knew that wasn't what I wanted to do.

*　　*　　*

Nan Hathaway.

That was her name, the waitress who told me I was a mutable sign. It's not the name she was born with, which was Polish and wouldn't look right on a marquee. She'd come to New York to be an actress or a singer or a dancer, and I'm not sure she cared which, so long as it led to her having her name—her new name—in lights. And, while we're dreaming, how about a nicer place to live than a West Forties rooming house on the wrong side of Ninth Avenue?

Meanwhile, she spent her days taking classes and going to open auditions, and her nights carrying a tray at Jimmy Armstrong's.

Her room was all right. Small, and in a run-down building, but it had its own bathroom, and a hotplate she could use to warm up a can of soup. She kept it neat.

We were never a couple, or even an item. This was early in my own stretch at Armstrong's, I was quits with my marriage and the NYPD, and just beginning to find my way into what I suppose I could call "adapting my professional talents to the private sector." Jimmy's joint was around the corner from my hotel, and it became my living room and my office, and was where I took most of my meals, and did most of my drinking.

I'm way ahead of myself here, but I might as well finish the thought, or the chain of thoughts.

We were friendly, Nan and I, and I liked her looks, and I guess she found mine tolerable. One night a look passed between us, not for the first time, and outside on Ninth Avenue I said I'd walk her home, and fell into step alongside her.

I read somewhere that there were two things you shouldn't tell in a memoir, how much money you made and who you slept with; unfortunately, it went on, those were the two subjects people were most interested in. I already broke the first rule when I told you what Perlstein paid me, but I don't expect to write more about money. I never cared all that much about it, which was just as well, as I was never destined to bring home a whole lot of it.

I broke the second rule, too, when I wrote about the consequences of knocking on Shirley's door in Parkchester. And I'll say now that Nan and I were in unspoken agreement as to how the evening would end. I didn't have to ask to go upstairs with her, and everything else followed as if we'd done it all before.

As we had, if not with each other.

I suppose we were together half a dozen times. Only one occasion might almost qualify as a date; she'd been given a pair of tickets to a workshop production of *The Play's the Thing*, the Ferenc Molnar comedy, and would I like to keep her company? I took her to dinner afterward and listened to her semiprofessional take on the performance we'd seen. The restaurant, long gone now, was Brittany du Soir, and we followed a light meal and bottle of wine with small snifters of brandy.

No, not brandy. A cordial. Drambuie, in fact.

Funny—or not funny—how I almost always remember what I drank.

We wound up at her place—the restaurant, at 53rd and Ninth, was halfway there. There was only one occasion when I took her back to my hotel room, and that was at her suggestion.

Her insistence, really. I was at Armstrong's, and she had the night off. If I'd been at my usual table I might have seen her come in, but I was at the bar with my back to the door, and wasn't aware of her until she was standing next to me, waving away the approaching bartender.

She said my name, just that. "Matthew," she said, although she always called me *Matt*. I read what I could in her face and got up from my stool, and she was already in motion, heading for the door.

Outside she asked if we could go to my place. We did, and without a word. The fellow behind the desk was professionally expressionless, but his face rarely showed much; he was always riding a light buzz of terpin hydrate and codeine, and I guess it must have worked for him, because I don't believe I ever once heard him cough.

My room was neat enough, but it could have been a mare's nest and I don't think she'd have noticed. When I closed the door and turned the lock she sighed, as if giving herself permission to relax.

She said, "Could you just fuck me? Could we make everything go away?"

Sometimes that's the point. Sometimes it's like whiskey, it's not the bouquet or the aroma, not the richness of the amber color, not the burn of raw moonshine or the complex peaty flavor of a premium single malt. Sometimes all those elements provide is assurance that the remedy is likely to work, that the drink will function as a solvent, smoothing and softening the sharp edges of the awful present moment.

That it—a drink or another person—will make everything go away.

I liked her enough to want to pour her this drink, as it were. And her charms were more than enough to make my role a labor of lust, if not of love. And so for a spell we couldn't get our fill of each other, and then we could and did.

I may have dropped off to sleep, but not for more than a few minutes, and when I opened my eyes she was on her feet and gathering her clothes. I said I'd walk her home, and she said I was sweet but not to be silly, that it was early and anyway she'd take a cab. I didn't argue, and when my eyelids dropped I didn't trouble to open them.

And that was that, and a day or two later we were friendly waitress and regular customer, the mixture as before. I had a case I was working, don't ask me which one, and it was heating up and getting more of my time and attention. And Nan was seeing somebody, most likely whoever it was whose behavior—brutal or distant or whatever it may have been—had been sufficiently upsetting to drive her to my bed.

We were together one more time. Her shift ended and she picked up a drink, a glass of red wine, and brought it over to my table, sat down and had a sip or two. Then she said she thought she owed me an apology. For what? For using me, she said. I assured her I'd had a good time, and that I'd never felt ill-used.

"Even so," she said, and giggled. What was so funny? "I was just thinking," she said, "that I picked you up like a dildo."

"I've been called worse," I said.

And then we were talking, and it was loose and easy. I finished my drink and she finished hers and we left the bar together and headed downtown. It had rained earlier, and it was still drizzling, but not enough to matter.

"This'll just be fun," she said.

And it was. It was also our last time together, and I think it was the last time I laid eyes on her. I spent much of the next few days in the Elmhurst section of Queens, where the proprietor of a diner on Queens Boulevard was pretty sure one of his cashiers had declared himself an unofficial partner. What complicated things was that my client had tried to prevent just this sort of thing by hiring relatives, and the leading suspect was a nephew on his wife's side of the family.

I don't remember the details, let alone the names. I had lots of cases like this, most of them easily solved, even if the parties weren't necessarily thrilled with the outcome. I think one of them, possibly this one, found its way into one of the books.

It doesn't matter. I could see right away that my guy's guess was right, and the motivator was either a heroin habit or gambling debts, and I can't remember which. I did what I did, and I got paid and went back to Manhattan, and to Armstrong's.

No Nan, and I asked the guy behind the stick if she'd been in. All he knew was she'd quit and he didn't know why. Someone else did; an audition had paid off, and she'd hurried off to join the road company of some play.

Gigs like that don't last forever. I figured she'd be back. And maybe she was, maybe she was waiting tables somewhere else, maybe she'd come home with a few extra dollars in her purse and found a nicer place to live. A studio apartment in Chelsea, say, a step up from a roach motel in Hell's Kitchen.

Switch neighborhoods in New York and your whole life changes. You have to find a new laundromat and a new dry cleaner, a new pizza stand and a new Chinese restaurant.

A new place to drink. New people to sleep with.

Funny. That last night, after our passage had indeed been fun, just as she'd predicted, she told me I could stay over. I don't know that she'd made the invitation before. As usual, though, I put on my clothes and walked home.

It had stopped raining, but the pavement was still damp and the air was fresher than usual, as if cleansed by the rain. I felt good, and found myself thinking of Nan and wondering if there was anything there for us.

Probably not.

If her name was ever in lights, I never saw it. Or in print, either. If, like most waitresses with dreams, she'd settled for a less glamorous life, she might well have returned to her original less-glamorous name.

I could probably track her down, and without leaving my desk. That's how most private investigators do most of their work these days. You can Knock On Doors without Getting Off Your Ass, and professionals can access subscription data bases that make it easy.

But toward what end?

*　　*　　*

How did I get so far off track?

*   *   *

From an email received this morning, in response to one I wrote last night:

"For God's sake, so what if the narrative's disjointed? Let it go where it goes. The sequence doesn't matter. This isn't a case report, it's just you putting down whatever comes to mind. What you want to do is let it flow without worrying what comes out of the faucet. So don't stop, and don't look back over your shoulder. When you're done we can decide if it needs editing.

"My guess is it won't need much. You're a good writer. Wasn't that what got you started on the track to a gold shield? All you have to do now is stay out of your own way.

"And no, I don't want to see what you've written, not until it's done. Don't send it to me. If you do I'll delete it unread. Don't show it to anybody, not even Elaine. And quit going back over it yourself. Trust the process. Trust yourself.

"What you want to do here is be the moving finger, and I know you remember the poem. You write and you move on . . ."

LB

Just like that.

And yes, I know the poem. *The Rubaiyat of Omar Khayyam,* and I didn't have to Google it to get the words right because we own a copy.

Here's the quatrain in question:

> *The moving finger writes; and, having writ,*
> *Moves on: nor all thy piety nor wit*
> *Shall lure it back to cancel half a line,*
> *Nor all thy tears wash out a word of it.*

Hard to argue with that.

*   *   *

While I was weighing the pluses and minuses of life as a union plumber, and the security that came with it, something made me think of Stan Gorski. I hadn't seen him since I walked away from the gym at St. Margaret's, and my only thoughts of him over the years were fleeting. On a construction job, it might occur to me that I was better at swinging a hammer or toting a bucket of joint compound for the hours I'd put in working the heavy bag.

Stan hadn't said much during training sessions, aside from urging me to step into a punch, that sort of thing. But one day I was standing alongside him, both of us watching a likely Golden Gloves entrant working the double-end bag, and from out of nowhere he started talking about being a cop, and how great it was.

"You wake up in the morning and know you're gonna spend your day making the city a little bit better than it'd be without you. You walk down the street and the good people are glad to see you and the bad ones are hoping they saw you before you saw them. Long as you do your job you're gonna get to keep that job, and you won't get rich but you won't miss any meals, either. And you won't ever want to hang it up, but when the time comes there's a decent pension waiting for you."

That's not word for word, but it's probably close.

And that's how it came back to me, while I was considering a life of opening drains.

*   *   *

I looked for him at St. Margaret's, but not everything stays the same forever, and I couldn't find anyone who remembered when a cop trained teen-age boxers in the school gym, let alone had a clue where the program might have moved to. I couldn't find him in the phone book, either. I decided it wasn't meant to be, and I let it go for a day, and then it occurred to me to go to the nearest precinct house.

I left a message, and a day or two later we were having a beer. The PAL program had found a new venue after whoever was in charge pulled St. Margaret's out from under them. "We had a colored kid come around, a lightweight, a lot of natural ability and he picked things up in a hurry. Nice young man, and he might have a career as a boxer, but he was the wrong color for the priest in charge. Not that the son of a bitch would come right out and say it. 'The wrong element,' was the phrase he used. The program was bringing the wrong element to the school. Now of course it was possible we could change the complexion of our program—and he gave me the side eye to underline the word 'complexion.'"

So they'd moved on, but by the time they found a new venue he'd lost his heart for it. I told him what was new in my life, and he was sorry to learn about my mother. I said I'd been steered toward the plumbing trade, and we talked about its merits, and I said, "Stan, the reason I got in touch—" and he said, "You're thinking it might be more satisfying to swing a nightstick than a pipe wrench. Am I right?"

I'd sought him out so that he could sell me on it, and he did. And he told me what I had to do, and when and where I had to do it, and I'm sure before I started at the Police Academy he called ahead to tell somebody I was worth looking out for.

It must have been three, four weeks in that the two of us got together for a beer, and he told me one of the instructors said I struck him as a kid with a future in the department. He dropped this in very casually, and he didn't say which instructor, but it was encouragement, and came at a good time. My own view of the matter tended to swing back and forth, from *I've found the life that was always meant for me* to *What the fuck am I doing here?*

In a sense that mental two-step—you could probably label it *bipolar* if you wanted to see it as pathological—never entirely stopped, but after that conversation with Stan my future was never in question. I was a cop, that was where I belonged, and however I felt about it was just a feeling.

Years later someone in an AA room said, "Feelings aren't facts," a phrase I was to hear again and again, in that room and others. But the first time I heard it I had a sense of recognition, as if it was something I'd long since learned and forgotten.

Something else I learned that day. The bond that led Stan to show up at my dad's funeral, and to initiate that first conversation about boxing, had been forged when Charlie Scudder got in a punch-up with some other drunk at one of his regular joints. Nobody went to the hospital, but it was enough of an incident that the cops were called, and Stan was one of the responding officers.

The next stop could have been Central Booking, but this guy Charlie was a guy Stan knew by sight, and if he'd been in trouble before Stan didn't know about it. He was a frequent customer at the bar with no history as a troublemaker, and it was unclear who'd started the fight, or what it was about. So Stan had used his judgment, and settled my dad down, and, after he got a cup of coffee into him, walked him home.

And they'd run into each other a couple of times after that. Friends? Probably not that, but friendly enough so that Stan had shown up at Gleason's.

Look at it in a certain light and you could say that it was my father's drinking that steered me to the NYPD, even as my own drinking floated me out of it. Sometimes I see it that way. More often, though, it all seems to me a matter of destiny. That all rivers go where they're meant to go, and that it's gravity that determines the direction of flow.

That sounds deeper than it is.

Never mind. There's a ceremony when a class graduates from the Police Academy, and family members generally attend. My parents were gone, obviously, and none of my other relatives showed up, though a few might have come by if it had occurred to me to tell anyone about it. But it hadn't, and they didn't.

Stan Gorski did. He came over after for a handshake and the predictable back-and-forth: *"See what you got me into?"* *"Hey, you look good in blue. Don't be too quick to disgrace that uniform, okay?"* Then he drifted away to talk to one of the instructors, and I wound up joining a couple of my classmates for drinks around the corner on Lexington Avenue.

I never saw him again.

We spoke a few times. I called him—a time or two for advice, but also just to report in. We talked about getting together. Every year there's a card of six or eight bouts, NYPD versus FDNY. *"Cops and firemen taking punches at each other, Matt, which is nothing new, but once a year they actually do it with gloves on."*

But we didn't go, and we lost touch, and I was already in plain-clothes when I overheard part of a stationhouse conversation: "And the priest kept saying Stanislaus, which I never knew was his name. I always thought it was Stanley."

I asked who they were talking about, and it was Stan, of course, and one of them had been to his funeral a day or two earlier. He'd been home alone, he'd lived alone for the past ten years, ever since his divorce, and he'd been cleaning his gun, and it discharged accidentally.

As noted, by the time this happened I was already out of the uniform, and a lot less green than the first time I put it on. So I knew that he hadn't been cleaning his gun, that something had moved him to put it in his mouth and pull the trigger.

I don't know why he ate his gun. Does anyone, including the featured performer, ever really know?

If I'd heard in time, I'd have been at his funeral. For all the good that would have done either of us.

*   *   *

What I remember most about the early days in my new blue uniform was how conscious I was of it when I was out in public. You put it on and you felt different, but even after you'd grown used to it, when your body took for granted the weight of the gun and the cuffs and the nightstick and the bulk of the pocket notebook, you still had to get used to the way people looked at you, and the way they tried not to look at you.

I was fortunate in that the uniform they gave me was the closest thing to a perfect fit. That's not always the case. There were at least two of my classmates who found a tailor to do a little nipping and tucking. Most of us made do with what we got, and in my case that was no hardship.

If I was self-conscious about my new blue suit, I was also pleased with how I looked in it. Posing in front of the mirror on my closet door, admiring my reflection. Well, it was sixty years ago. If I want to be embarrassed about the man I was back then, that touch of closed-door narcissism is the least of it.

No question the uniform changed the way citizens looked at me; it also changed the way I looked at them. Staring was no longer something to apologize for. It was now my job to look at the people around me, to size them up, to get a sense of what was going on and what might happen next. Anyone in my field of vision might collapse and need my help, or draw a weapon and need my quick response.

By the time a new patrolman gets used to being in uniform, he's generally looking forward to getting out of it. Most never do, not until they put in their papers and start drawing their pensions, and that's true even for most of the men who move up the ranks. Desk sergeants and lieutenants are uniformed officers, and even the top brass spend most of their on-duty hours wearing blue, albeit their uniforms have been tarted up with a few yards of gold braid.

My first post was temporary, filling in at a precinct in Queens that was a few men short. They had me walking a beat and functioning as an over-qualified school crossing guard, and I was just beginning to get the hang of it when I was given a permanent assignment to the 78th Precinct in Brooklyn, and partnered with a veteran patrolman named Vincent Mahaffey.

I'd spent most of my life in the Bronx, and the rest of it in Queens, and I'd ventured into Manhattan enough to find my way around, especially in the part of it where numbered streets and avenues kept it simple. So of course they posted me to Brooklyn.

Well, that's where Vince was, at the Seven-Eight, and had been ever since they gave him a badge and a gun. And I've come to believe he's what got me a posting in Park Slope. Because there were a couple of cops, starting with Stan Gorski and including one or two of my instructors at the academy, who evidently saw something in me.

That I'd make a decent cop, I guess. And something else—that I might have the potential for more than pounding a beat and twirling a nightstick.

If I did, it would show up way quicker with Mahaffey as a senior partner. He'd supply a rich postgraduate education, teaching me the things they hadn't gotten around to on East Twentieth Street.

I'd also be learning lessons they'd just as soon have me skip, but that was part of the package, wasn't it?

* * *

I know Vince is in some of the books. They don't get underway until I've put in my papers and walked out on my wife and kids and found a hotel room at Fifty-seventh and Ninth and pretty much settled into an essentially unsettled existence.

By then I'd largely lost touch with Vince. I'd left him and the Slope behind when they gave me a gold shield and assigned me to the Sixth Precinct, which was on Charles Street in the West Village. (It moved to a newer building a couple of blocks away on West Tenth, but by then I'd given the gold shield back to them. And the old Charles Street stationhouse got a gut re-hab and a new life as an upscale apartment house. With a new name, Le Gendarme.)

So Vince wasn't a part of my post-NYPD life, but in some of the books I refer back to incidents when I was still on the job, and I know he came up a few times. The seasoned cop, with a dark view of the world around him and the people who live in it, and a sense of rough justice that doesn't always go by the book.

I suppose that's fair enough. Vince taught me what the rules were, and which ones you had to follow if anybody was looking.

This was a long time ago, and while I've always prided myself on my memory, in recent years it's dimmed a bit, and I've come to regard it as unreliable. There are incidents of which I have no recollection, although it's indisputable that they occurred, and there are others for which my memory has proved artful, doing some editing and rewriting.

I remember my first meeting with Vince, and the look on his face as he took my measure. There was skepticism, and a de-gree of relief—I stood up straight, I didn't drool, I was the right color. Maybe I'd turn out to be all right, maybe I'd even do him some good. Time would tell.

Early on, there was a test. We were an hour or two into our shift when he pulled over to the curb, right behind a panel truck with two wheels on the street and two up on the sidewalk. Two men were unloading it, stacking cartons on the sidewalk, and the store owner was holding a clipboard and checking off items as he noted their presence.

He looked up at the two of us in our uniforms, recognized Vince. "I know," he said.

"Course you do," Vince said. "The whole block's a No Standing zone, plus he's half in the street and half on the sidewalk, which is a violation itself. Plus half the sidewalk's blocked with boxes."

There was a little back and forth, with a pro forma feel to it. I remember the place of business as a neighborhood housewares and hardware store, as common in its day as a nail salon or tattoo parlor now. The owner said he couldn't control delivery times, that he had to have goods on his shelves, that everybody with a pushcart knew you couldn't do business from an empty wagon. And his helper was late, what could you do, kids today, but as soon as he got here the cartons would be shifted inside where they wouldn't block traffic, and as soon as the delivery was completed the truck and its driver would go back where they came from, and what was a man supposed to do?

And Vince told the man he was right, he was a hundred percent right, but the law was the law, and it said to move the truck along now and write out a summons, and what was *he* supposed to do?

The man thrust his hands into his pockets and said he'd get the sidewalk clear as quickly as he possibly could. And the truck on its way. And Vince said that was reasonable, and things generally worked out when a couple of reasonable men had a chance to talk it out.

And they shook hands, and we got back in our squad car, and Vinnie pulled away from the curb and said, "See, that's an important lesson. Here's an incident that's a definite violation, no question. You got a truck parked where it's not supposed to be, blocking the street *and* the sidewalk, and you got boxes strewn out all over the sidewalk, and it's not like they're gonna disappear in five minutes. Other hand, here's a decent fellow just trying to make a living, running a small retail business that's an asset to the neighborhood, and what's *he* supposed to do? You go by the book, his delivery's interrupted, his shelves are full of empty spaces, plus he has to make an appearance downtown and pay whatever the fine is. You see what I mean?"

I said I did.

"You're a cop, you don't want that. But you can't drive on by and overlook it, either. You have to stop, you have to have the conversation we just had, and it won't make the truck or the boxes vanish in a puff of smoke, but they'll be out of the picture sooner than if we took no notice and kept driving. Make sense to you?"

Perfect sense, I said.

"They can't teach it at the Academy," he said, "but it's something they all know. You gotta know what's in the book, and you also gotta know when to leave the book on the shelf, when to use your judgment."

We talked some more, and he drove some more, and then he pulled to the curb and cut the engine. He drew a wallet from his pocket, found a ten-dollar bill, and handed it to me.

I figured I was supposed to pick up something, but the store we were parked in front of sold plumbing supplies, and I'd let that potential career go by the boards when I took the NYPD exam. I was puzzled, and my face must have shown it.

"When we shook hands," Vince said levelly, "his hand had a twenty-dollar bill in it. That there's your share."

* * *

That was the test. If I'd shown shock or gone into judgment, if I'd refused to take my portion of the bribe, he'd have found a way to cover. Knowing Vince, he'd have most likely passed it off as a gag; there'd been no twenty dollars from the store owner, and he was just trying to see what I was made of, whether the nuns would be proud of me.

(He knew I hadn't gone to Catholic school, and wasn't even Catholic in the first place, but that was a phrase he liked. "*Oh, wouldn't the nuns be proud of you!*")

And I might have bought it and I might not, but over the next month or two he'd find a way to dump me as a partner. He had his own way of doing things, and the pay he drew from his city job was by no means the extent of his income. The twenty-dollar handshake, in one form or another, put food on his table and new shoes on his kids' feet. He wasn't in any gangster's pocket, and he drew a ragged line between clean and dirty graft, but he couldn't live the life he'd chosen with a straight arrow for a partner.

Did any of this go through my mind at the time? I don't see how it could have. He hadn't said *Take your time now, think it over.* What he'd said was *That there's your share.*

What I did was take the money. What I said was thanks.

* * *

And what did I think about it?

Hard to say. I was, to a degree, the kind of straight arrow that would have worried Vince—or at least I had been. If I wasn't exactly shocked to discover that Eddie Towns was filling out questionnaires for people he hadn't bothered to interview, I was certainly taken aback, and in no hurry to take the same short-cut myself.

And I didn't show up for class on East Twentieth Street in the hope that they'd teach me how to steal. I may not have been wearing rose-colored glasses, but I still saw myself as very much on the side of the angels. I'd be able to spend my life, or at least the next twenty of thirty years of it, doing my part to make the city a better place. I'd be helping out good people and locking up bad people, and that struck me as a higher calling than plugging leaks and opening drains—although, now that I think about it, one's not a bad metaphor for the other.

So what did I think?

So that's how it works. I had ten dollars I hadn't had a few minutes ago, and the man who'd handed it to me was a little more relaxed in my presence, and I'd learned something about him even as he'd learned something about me. But the lesson I'd learned seemed to me to be less about my new partner and more about my new job. This was how it worked. This was how a store owner managed to take care of his business, and this was how a police officer managed to balance out conflict-ing realities.

If Vince Mahaffey felt more at ease with me once I took the money, well, it worked both ways. I felt a bond, because we'd shared something, and I sensed that he'd taught me something, and it was by no means the last of the things he had to teach me.

And, you know, I must have felt a touch of guilt. Because when I took the money I'd broken both a rule and a law, and none of that was customary behavior for me.

When our shift ended, Vince wrote up his report of the day's activity. The store owner and the delivery truck got a sentence or two, stating that we'd come upon a delivery to a specific retail establishment that was blocking traffic and secured the cooperation of all parties in rectifying the situation.

Close enough.

And the two of us went from the stationhouse to a bar he liked, something with Emerald in its name, and he bought the first round and I bought the second. Nowadays that would have pretty much accounted for my ten-dollar windfall, certainly in Park Slope. But everything was cheaper back then, booze included, and the pre-gentrification Slope was a working-class neighborhood with prices to match.

So I got change back from my ten-spot, and walked out of there with it in my pocket, because it wasn't the kind of place where anybody felt the need to tip the guy behind the stick. Leave your change on the bar at the Emerald Garden and they'd figure you were in a blackout.

Two drinks had me feeling good—no surprise there—and I might have stayed for a third. But I had a date.

* * *

Her name was Anita Rembauer, and I don't suppose I'd ever have met her if I hadn't tried to get a date with a friend of hers.

I was at the Police Academy, a few weeks into the training, and when they cut us loose I went around the corner with a couple of fellow trainees to a coffee shop on Third Avenue. I don't remember who I was with, but I excused myself when I glanced at a nearby table and saw a girl I recognized.

A woman, I suppose, because she'd been a year behind me at James Monroe, and I think we'd been in a class together. Biology? One of the sciences, anyway. I remembered her name was Corinne, though that may not be how she spelled it, and that she was on the swim team, which saddled her with Chlorine as a nickname. This didn't seem to bother her. Few things did, she was a sunny girl, and a pretty one.

Enough so that I carried my Coke over to her table. She remembered me right away and invited me to sit down, and she told me she worked in the neighborhood, and had stayed late in the office that night, and I said I was spending most of my evenings at the Academy. She hadn't even known it was in the neighborhood, but she thought it was terrific that I was going to become a cop, and I thought *she* was terrific, and when the moment seemed right I asked her if she might like to go to a movie that weekend.

Her face clouded, and she explained that she couldn't. She had a steady boyfriend, in fact they were the next thing to engaged. I was disappointed but hardly devastated, and I said I was sure they'd be very happy together, but if by some chance it didn't work out—

That got the kind of laugh that deepened my disappointment, and the announcement that she knew a girl she thought I'd like, one she was dead certain would like me. Her name was Anita, she worked two desks away in the same office, and she was cute and had a great sense of humor.

But there was one thing. Did I still live in the Bronx?

"She doesn't like Bronx boys? What is it, the accent?"

The problem, Corinne explained, was geographic in nature. Anita lived with her parents in Bensonhurst, deep in Brooklyn, and it took her a couple of trains and upwards of forty-five minutes to get to work in the morning. And Corinne, who'd lived not too far from me in the Bronx, had moved to a furnished room on East Eighteenth Street once she'd settled into her job, because her own commute had been almost that bad.

"So with you in the Bronx and her in Bensonhurst—"

The point was clear enough. We'd be spending all our time in transit.

But evidently the impulse to serve as matchmaker to one's friends, or even one's acquaintances, is a primal one. Corinne, having taken note of the problem, was quick to wave it away. Anita and I could certainly meet at a movie theater in Manhattan, she said, some spot equally convenient or inconvenient for both of us, and afterward if we hit it off we could have a drink or a bite to eat at some nearby restaurant, and then I could walk her to the subway and we could go our separate ways. How did that sound?

I said it sounded okay.

And that Saturday night I waited for her in front of the Criterion Theater, at Broadway and Forty-fourth. The picture, ideal to take a date to, starred Rock Hudson and Doris Day in what would now be called a rom-com. We'd spoken on the phone, and I'd told her I'd be wearing a cape and carrying a see-through plastic bag with a goldfish in it. She assured me she'd be easy to spot, that there weren't that many girls who shaved their heads.

We found each other with no trouble. Her hair, a rich brown, was in a ponytail, and her oval face was pretty. She was on the tall side, just a couple of inches shorter than I. I can't say we felt as though we'd known each other forever, but we were encouragingly at ease on first meeting. I'd already bought our tickets, and on the way in I picked up popcorn, and we found seats and watched the movie.

Afterward we had clam rolls and iced tea at the Howard Johnson's two blocks from the theater. It's long gone, but so are Rock and Doris. And so's the Criterion, for that matter, which morphed into a Toys-R-Us around the turn of the century, and is now something else.

Nothing stays the same.

* * *

I had a good time, and so did she, and we walked the half-dozen blocks to the Times Square subway station in a mixed mood. In the ordinary course of things we'd be planning other dates, but it wasn't much of a stretch to say that Brooklyn and the Bronx were poles apart.

I offered to escort her home, and she told me that was sweet but not to be ridiculous, and she'd be fine on the subway and her neighborhood was safe and well-lit. I did walk her to her platform, and then went off in search of mine.

I said I'd call her, but doesn't everybody says that?

And then a week or so later I ran into Corinne on my way to

class. Anita had really had a good time, she said, and had commented on how bright and good-looking I was. "Although I must say I never noticed it myself," she said.

It seems to me that Corinne married that virtual fiancé of hers, but I never learned whether it worked out or whatever became of her. I can only hope that, married or single, she found her way into sales, because she had a gift. We had that brief conversation on the sidewalk in front of the Academy, and the next day I called Anita and asked her if there was anything interesting two people could find to do in Bensonhurst. And how did you get there, anyway?

By subway, of course, and if you started from the Bronx, as I was to do two nights later, you'd have to change trains at least once. We arranged to meet at her neighborhood movie house, and I allowed for plenty of travel time and got there early. There was a bar two doors down from the theater, and I'd have liked a beer, but instead I remembered something I'd heard in one of my classes on Twentieth Street and stayed on the street, walking around as if this were my beat, sizing things up, letting my eyes take the measure of the scene around me.

Another thing Yogi Berra probably never said was that you can observe a lot just by watching, and I was putting that notion to the test, running a silent monologue in the privacy of my mind. *That kid looks wrong for the neighborhood. What's he looking for? Why does that woman keep looking at her watch? Older man's walking very deliberately, setting each foot down very carefully. Physically frail? Or maybe trying hard not to look as drunk as he is?*

And then: *Jesus, there's a nice-looking girl.* And the realization, maybe half a second after the thought, that it was Anita, and that her eyes were working the street because she was looking for me.

The movie was okay, and so was the pizza place around the corner. We each had a slice and a Coke, and talked long enough to eat and drink our way through a second round. Our conversation was easy, and not overly burdened with substance. High school, friends getting married, favorite TV programs—nothing we couldn't have phoned in. I said the pizza was good, and she said I could count on her to find good pizza, a nice Italian girl like herself.

Oh? Rembauer?

German on her father's side, Italian on her mother's. She pronounced it Eye-talian, for effect.

"The ideal combination," I said. "Our traditional allies. I just hope you've got a Japanese aunt."

That could have fallen terribly flat, as I realized halfway through. But her reaction was a bark of delighted laughter, and the way we looked at each other was different after that exchange. She liked that I'd said what I said, that I'd had the thought and voiced it, and I liked that she'd laughed.

Years later, when some optimist opened a sushi restaurant in Syosset, the two of us had dinner there. This wasn't long after our move from Brooklyn, and sushi was pretty much a new thing throughout the New York area, although I gather it was already part of the landscape in California. I'd had it a couple of times in the Theater District, a few blocks from Midtown North, and after the usual banter ("Hey, is this a restaurant or a bait shop?") I discovered, as most people do, that I liked it.

But it was Anita's first taste of raw fish, and I wasn't sure she'd take to it, and expressed relief when she did. "Well, what did you expect?" she said. "Don't tell me you forgot all about my Japanese aunt."

*   *   *

By then, of course, it had already gone sour.

*   *   *

Nine words. *By then of course it had already gone sour.* Nine words typed out in that particular order, then deleted, then typed again. With commas, without commas. Deleted, reworded, restored, and so on.

Nine words. Command + Save, and Quit Word, and Shut Down, and boot up this morning and here they are, just as they were.

I don't want to write about Anita. She's dead, she died twenty years ago. I'd gone to the funeral, I'd followed the other cars out to the cemetery and watched from a distance as they buried her. She spent ten years as my wife, and they weren't all bad but they became more bad than good. After the split and the divorce she stayed on in the house in Syosset and raised the boys and made do on what money I managed to send her. And she met and married Graham Thiele, and he was a much better husband for her than I'd ever been, and then one day she had a heart attack and was gone, and I sat in my car at a Long Island cemetery and watched them lower her casket into the ground.

"You must go on. I can't go on. I'll go on."

That's Beckett, of course. The line everybody knows, except I had to look it up to get it right.

He never says why.

*　　*　　*

Back to Bensonhurst. We finished our pizza and I walked her the eight or ten blocks to her house. Her father owned the three-story row house, and he and his wife and four children lived on the ground floor. He'd installed his mother and an unmarried sister on the second floor, and an elderly Italian widower rented the top floor.

The house had been recently painted, and I would learn that George Rembauer painted it himself, a task he performed once a year. He took good care of his property, you could see that at a glance.

We kept up an easy conversation most of the way to her house, but ran out of words in the last block or so. Then "I had a nice time, Matt," and "So did I," and a moment that was only medium-awkward, and then a kiss, which turned out to be a little more than perfunctory.

If she'd lived alone, I think she'd have invited me in.

Instead she went inside and I walked a half mile to the subway and spent the next two hours getting home to the Bronx. For the first half hour or so I was in the warm afterglow of a very enjoyable evening, and then that wore off as I faced the fact that I would probably never see her again, because what was the point? She and I weren't all that far apart, but you couldn't say the same for Brooklyn and the Bronx.

Then they gave me my badge and my gun, and stuck me in the Middle Village section of Queens. That was almost as remote as Bensonhurst, and even though I knew it was temporary and my next slot could be anywhere in the five boroughs, I didn't waste any time finding a furnished room within walking distance of the stationhouse. It cost me eighteen dollars a week, which is no money now and wasn't much money then, and when they switched me to a more permanent slot at the Seven-Eight in Park Slope, I found something a little nicer and not much more expensive on Garfield Place.

At the end of the month I returned the keys to my landlord in the Bronx. I stuffed everything I wanted to keep into two suitcases and gave everything else to Goodwill. Goodbye Bronx, hello Brooklyn—and within the week I picked up a phone.

"Hi, this is Matt," I said. "Matt Scudder. I'm sorry I haven't called, but things have been busy. I've got a new blue uniform, and you'll never guess where I'm living."

She got to see the place for herself. She met me after work at a restaurant someone had recommended, and I don't remember what we ate, but we drank a bottle of wine with it.

Afterward, I told her we were only a few blocks from my apartment. Would she like to see it?

"I thought you said it was a furnished room."

"It's one room," I said, "and they supplied the furniture. But my partner told me to call it a studio apartment. He said a furnished room sounds like I'm on welfare. What's so funny?"

"Well, it sort of does."

"Besides," I said, "I've got my own private bathroom."

"God, I wish I did. I've got two sisters and a brother. Your studio apartment sounds like heaven."

*   *   *

We'd get together once or twice a week. While we never officially established Saturday night as a date night, it became essentially that; unless something else got in the way, we'd spend Saturday evening together. And, maybe half the time, some weekday evening as well.

I'd pick her up at her house—it wasn't too long before I'd met her family, one person at a time—or we'd meet at a neighborhood movie house or restaurant. A couple of times we rode into Manhattan together, once when Mahaffey passed on tickets someone had given him to a Broadway show, *Enter Laughing*. All I remember about it is that it was funny, and that an audience laughed differently at a live performance than at a movie.

Our evenings always wound up on Garfield Place, and two or three times they started there; I'd call her at the end of my shift, we'd meet at my apartment and go straight to bed, and we'd get something to eat after.

Before I made the move to Brooklyn, I'd led what I suppose was a normal enough life for a man my age and in my position. There'd been a couple of girls I'd gone out with enough times that the sex act was a natural consequence, and once we'd managed that we seemed to be done with one another. And I don't want to forget a woman a few years older than I, a regular at a bar two blocks from my house; for years I would think of her every time I heard the song "Queen of the Silver

Dollar." There were three nights when I was the one who got to take her home, and it was always an uncomplicated good time, but that was all it ever was or would be.

So it's safe to say Anita was my first relationship. I don't know what I thought we were doing, exactly, but it was clear that we were doing it together.

And I suppose I was her first relationship.

It depends, I suppose, on how you keep score. She kept steady company her senior year in high school with a classmate at New Utrecht High, a boy whose first name I'd been told but have long since forgotten. They'd have long make-out sessions that were as frustrating as they were exciting, and that might well have led to intercourse if they hadn't managed to discover hand jobs. That took the pressure off—well, some of it—and they talked about going all the way, and it was something they knew they'd get to eventually, but instead he went to college at Stony Brook and that was the end of that. They ran into each other once when he was home for Christmas or spring break, whenever it was, and found themselves with nothing to say.

I suppose you'd have to call that a relationship, but because they did not in fact go all the way, it would go in the record book with an asterisk.

Going all the way. Jesus, the world was different then.

And in fact she did go all the way once, almost a year before Corinne played matchmaker, and that was the farthest thing from a relationship. At the time it was a clear case of caddish behavior, and nowadays it wouldn't be a stretch to call it date rape. A man she'd never met picked her up at a party where she'd already had a little too much to drink, and managed to get a couple more drinks inside her, and took her to the Seth Low playground just off Bay Parkway and got her skirt up and her panties down.

And so on, and she was either passed out or in a blackout, because when she came to an hour or so later she knew what had to have happened but didn't have any real memory of it.

Until she told me this, one night on Garfield Place, she'd never said a word about it to anyone. Who could she tell, and what could she say? Early on she was terrified he might have gotten her pregnant, and was hugely relieved when that proved not to be the case, and once she was able to relax about that, all she wanted to do was forget the whole thing. She didn't know his name or anything about him beside the fact that he was a son of a bitch, and she wasn't sure she'd recognize him if she saw him again, and hoped she'd never find out.

I'd known she wasn't a virgin, but hearing what had happened let me see myself as the only man in her life. The boyfriend didn't count because all he ever got was a hand job, and Mr. Date Rape didn't count because she hadn't had much say in the matter. So I was her first, really, her first and only, and knowing this probably made it that much more inevitable that we'd wind up getting married.

For a while, I had the occasional fantasy of encountering the fellow. I imagined us walking down the street, and a startled Anita clutching my arm: "That's him! That's him!"

And so on.

He never did turn up, and the fantasy itself faded before too long. With time, my view of the incident has gone through changes. At first I saw it all one way: he was a bad man who'd done a bad thing, and more than deserved whatever punishment I might fantasize handing him.

But how exceptional was his behavior, really? "*I seen my opportunities and I took 'em,*" as an old Tammany Hall hack said, talking about the graft he regarded as an entitlement. And wasn't it at least as natural for a man to take note of a woman who'd had too much to drink—and to see his opportunity and take it?

Over the years, God knows there were women I slept with who'd had a lot to drink, though not often more than I'd had myself. On at least one occasion, during the years after my marriage ended and before I got sober, my partner *du noir* had been in a blackout, although there was no way I could have known it at the time, and when she awoke she admitted she had no idea who I was or what we'd done.

Still, she didn't seem traumatized, or even rueful. Or in a hurry to get up and get on with her life, and in fact we stayed in bed another half hour, and she said, "Now this way I'll have something to remember."

Was that date rape?

Maybe. I don't know. Standards evolve over time. A few centuries back, rape involving actual physical force was often labeled *gallantry,* especially when the gallant was of a higher social class than his victim. And, while it might be the sort of behavior one hoped a young man would outgrow, well, boys will be boys, won't they? And shouldn't she have known better than to be alone with him? Really, what did she expect?

Different times. I read somewhere that the swoon originated

as a means for a woman to make herself available to a suitor without acting like a slut.

*   *   *

George Washington Plunkitt. That was the Tammany guy who saw and took his opportunities. A hard name to forget, and no wonder it came back to me.

*   *   *

One other thought, and then I can turn the page on Anita's virginity and the loss thereof. It was years later, when we were well settled in Syosset, that I wondered if she'd been telling the truth.

Because it was a handy way to explain her loss of virginity. Not that I required an explanation, not that I'd have been likely to ask for one.

Still, she might have felt it was a way to tie off a loose end. Maybe she didn't want to say that her high school boyfriend had gotten more than manual satisfaction, maybe there'd been another fellow in the picture she didn't care to admit to. Easy enough to make up an opportunistic stranger, conveniently nameless, a man she'd never seen before and would never see again. And the act itself? Well, she couldn't remember it, and was very likely unconscious at the time, so it was almost as if it never happened.

But let's give her the benefit of the doubt. Who cares what truths she might have shaded, or what untold adventures she might have had before I met her, or even after? She wasn't perfect, but she was a better wife than I was a husband, and a far better mother than I was a father.

Jesus, the woman's dead.

I didn't want to start writing about her. I'd a lot rather write about Mahaffey.

*   *   *

Vincent Mahaffey.

I'd a lot rather write about Mahaffey, I wrote, and now I can't find a way to get started. It was as his partner that I learned how to be a cop, and truly became one. They taught me enough at the Academy to make me qualified to wear a uniform, and my fill-in assignment in Middle Village enabled me to wear it with a certain amount of confidence, but until Vince got ahold of me I wasn't really there yet.

Much of what I learned at his side I'd have learned from any veteran officer. How to look at a street scene, how to make sense of what I saw there. How to ask questions, and when to wait through a silence for the next response, and when to push, and when to let it go.

How to access your instincts, and how far to trust them.

You couldn't learn this in a classroom, or out of a book. You could only pick it up on the job, and if you were doing the job right you couldn't help picking it up. But who they partnered you with made a big difference in what you learned and how well you learned it.

The first thing he taught me was how to drive a car. I sort of knew, I'd had occasion while working construction to get behind the wheel of a car or small truck and move it to a better spot or run a short errand. I'd even filled out a form and picked up a learner's permit once, shortly after I turned sixteen, but I never did anything with it. I never had a lesson, formal or informal, and a vehicle with standard transmission was a challenge; I could get it from Point A to Point B, but not very smoothly.

I remembered a couple of cars my father had owned, but that was all before the shoe store failed, well before I reached driving age. I wasn't about to go buy a car, so what did I need with a license? I figured it was something I'd get around to sooner or later, but I was in no rush.

Our first day in the squad car, Vince drove. An hour or two into our shift we stopped for coffee, and when we got back to the car he tossed me the keys. I explained, in a couple of quick sentences, that I didn't have a license, or any real experience behind the wheel. He thought about it, said it was no problem, retrieved the keys and drove around until a radio call gave us a place to go.

The next morning, he tossed me the keys again. I started to say something and he held up a hand that cut me off in mid-sentence. I knew how to start an engine, didn't I? And how to pull away from a curb?

But I didn't have a license, I said.

"And that's a violation," he said. "Driving without a license, but who's gonna pull us over and ask to see yours?"

I started up, pulled away from the curb, headed off down the avenue. Braked for a red light, waited for the green, kept driving. Turned right when he said to turn right, left when he said left.

"You know how to drive," he said after we'd gone maybe a

dozen blocks. "You're not easy with it yet, but that'll come soon enough. Same as everything else on the job, what you start out knowing in your head needs some time to get down into your bones. A week or two and we'll see about getting you a license."

Okay.

"Meantime," he said, "try not to hit anything. Especially a nun. You run over a nun in an Irish neighborhood and you just know some prick'll want to see your license."

*   *   *

I didn't hit anything, and I guess I did know how to drive, in my head if not yet in my bones. I'd been in enough cars driven by other people, and paid enough attention, and I guess Yogi was right about this as well; I had observed a lot by watching. And I had Vince in the car, and while he may have been casual about it, part of his attention was always on my driving, and he'd let me know when I did something wrong.

Early on I'd picked up a new Learner's Permit at DMV, so it wasn't entirely illegal for me to be driving as long as I had a licensed driver in the car, although I'm sure it went against department regulations. And one day a couple of weeks in he had me drive to Marine Park, where he knew an older guy named Leo who road-tested applicants. I got to jump the line, and Leo took Vince's place in the passenger seat and told me to turn left and turn right and pull up next to a particular car and parallel park behind it.

And so on. He had a clipboard but I never saw him look at it or make any notes, and when we were back where we'd started he told Vince I did fine. "It's all experience," he said, "and Matt here's had some, and it shows. Ninety-some percent of what I get is high school kids, and I got a policy I keep to myself of failing any kid who's taking the test for the first time. He don't have to do anything wrong. He can do everything right and he's still short on experience, so let him and his dad go practice some more, and the second time around he'll pass. Matt, you already took the written test, right?"

I hadn't known there was one.

He had a form and gave it the top spot on his clipboard. "Here you go. Ten questions, and six right is a passing grade."

I hadn't studied, but a glance at the questions made it clear this wasn't a test you had to study for. I did get one question wrong, something about braking distance, but the rest of the answers struck me as self-evident. I remember one true-or-false question: *In a three-lane highway, the middle lane is used for parking.*

I asked Leo if anybody ever failed the written test. "You'd be surprised," he said.

*   *   *

I suppose you'd have to say he was a racist. Not the way George Wallace was a racist, not the way the white supremacists are racists. But for Vince Mahaffey there was a line drawn through the human race, and white people were on one side of it and everybody else was on the other.

On the job, he treated people pretty much the same irrespective of their color. If two men of different races got into it and we were called to the scene, he didn't automatically assume the white guy was in the right. But he noticed the difference, he was always aware of it, and I'm sure the black people with whom he had contact were aware of his awareness.

If he spotted a young black male in a predominantly white neighborhood, he paid attention. He'd keep an eye on the guy, and if something triggered his cop instincts he might take the next step. You have to honor those instincts and act on them, you can't do the job right if you don't, but there's always the question of just how much something like skin color serves to give shape and focus to one's instincts.

Did he ever use the N-word?

No, but in all the years I carried a badge I don't think I heard the word come out of a cop's mouth more than half a dozen times, and the men involved were drunk and off-duty. One lesson they leaned on hard at the Academy was that racial and ethnic slurs had no place in an officer's vocabulary.

That wasn't enough to change your attitudes and perceptions, but it set limits on how you talked about them.

And you could always figure out a work-around. I never heard Vince say the N-word, but he made frequent use of another N-word.

Of a description of two men seen fleeing from the scene of a liquor store robbery: "Turns out it was a couple of Norwegians. How's that for a surprise?"

Vince wasn't the only cop to employ *Norwegian* as a code word for African-American. He'd started out at the Six-Eight in Bay Ridge, where the bulk of the city's Norwegian population lived, mostly around Ovington Avenue. I'm sure some of them got drunk and beat their wives, and I don't doubt that a few of them committed felonies and shot drugs, but by and large they were a stereotypically law-abiding lot. So referring to black criminals as Norwegians was a way to avoid sounding like a racist, and ironic in the bargain.

* * *

I remember a call we got. It couldn't have been early on in our partnership, because we'd already made the switch to plain-clothes. A burglary in progress on President Street, and the call wasn't entirely accurate because the burglar had quit the prem-ises before the homeowners returned home to find their front door ajar.

They'd done what you're supposed to do, which is call it in and wait outside, and they were waiting for us on the porch of a three-story frame house. They looked like what they were, a professional couple in their early thirties, spending their free time converting a triplex into a one-family home. They both wore glasses, to slightly different effect; he looked like a book-worm and she looked like a hot librarian.

They hadn't heard any sounds within, he told us, and he figured whoever broke in was long gone, but—

Vince told him he'd done the right thing, and we stepped past them and went in with drawn guns. That felt foolish, because you knew the house was empty, but at the same time you were on edge, because what if it wasn't?

We checked all three floors, and I remember the incident now and then when Elaine's watching one of her house shows on HGTV, because it was a renovation in progress. Back on the porch, we told the couple they could go on in, and maybe they could take a quick look around and see what was missing.

"Gonna be hard to tell," the husband said. "Place is a work in progress, and progress is slow when you do it yourselves. Some day it'll be straight out of *House Beautiful*, but when we left this morning the place was a mess."

Vince told him that much hadn't changed, but why didn't they have a look around? While they did, we waited on the porch and wondered if they might have bitten off more than they could chew. "Imagine doing all of that yourself," I said, "and living in the place while you're doing it."

An older man had paused on the sidewalk, and Vince walked over and asked him if lived in the neighborhood and if he'd noticed anything earlier in the day. Like what? Like somebody on the porch, or trying the door.

"I mind my own business," the fellow said. "I got no particular interest in these people."

Right.

The homeowners came back to report that, as far as they could tell, the forced door was the only indication anybody had been in the house. If anything was missing, they hadn't noted its absence. Vince said they could take their time and file a burglary report for insurance purposes at leisure, but it looked like a kid or kids wanting a peek inside, and running off once their curiosity had been satisfied.

"At any rate," Vince said, "not a professional burglar. You have any trouble with your neighbors?"

A frown. "What kind of trouble?"

"I don't know. Anybody you might have had words with,

anybody who might not have neighborly feelings toward the two of you?"

"And why would that be?"

"Hey, no reason," Vince said. "There's questions we're taught to ask when there's been a break-in. Nothing important."

"Just routine," the man said levelly.

"That's it."

Back in the car, he said, "'And why would that be?' Jesus, you're as black as the ace of spades and your wife's all blond hair and blue eyes, and the two of you just bought your way into the middle of a white working-class neighborhood and booted out some long-term residents so you can fill all three floors with half-breed pickaninnies."

"It's probably just as well you didn't say that."

"What's the difference? That's what he thinks he heard." And, a few minutes later, "I wonder if I'll ever get used to it."

"People with an attitude?"

"That much I'm already used to. When you're a cop everybody you meet's got an attitude. No, the other."

I knew what he meant. I'd probably known all along.

"You see it more and more, but not in the Slope, not in a white neighborhood in Brooklyn. Greenwich Village, Times Square, wherever you got your actors and artists. If I ran into the two of them in some hippy coffeehouse on Macdougal Street, would I react the same as on a front porch on President Street?"

He answered his own question. "Probably not, but I'd still take notice of them. But less than I would have five years ago. The more you run into it, the less impact. Like anything else in life, like a fucking Beetle."

He lost me there. A ladybug? Ringo Starr?

"A VW, a Volkswagen. When people first started driving them, you took notice every time you saw one. Now you pay about as much attention as when it's a Ford or a Chevy. They're all over the place, they're just part of the landscape."

I said something about VWs and mileage, and we talked a little about cars, and then he said, "So what's your take on the break-in?"

"When nothing was missing," I said, "I wondered for a minute if maybe the lock failed to engage when they left the house. But someone had definitely forced the door."

"Somebody with some kind of pry bar, with a little brute force to back it up. I thought kids, but I don't think so. This was somebody who didn't exactly know how to jimmy a lock, but he knew how to try."

"So a neighbor?"

He nodded. "Not kids and not a pro, so that's what's left. Somebody who doesn't want a black guy living on the same block, especially one with a white wife. I think the break-in was to send a message."

"That would fit with leaving the door ajar. 'No, you didn't forget to lock up. You locked it and I opened it, and I can do that anytime I want to.'"

"Something like that. You know what I think? I think he might have had ideas of trashing the place, and one look told him not to bother. The best way to make their lives miserable was to leave everything the way he found it."

"When they finally finish—"

He shook his head. "Never happen. He works and she works, and I can't swear to it but my guess is she's got a bun in the oven. There's a little roundness to her belly that doesn't completely go with the rest of her. Both of them working and she's pregnant, and they've got a disaster area covering three floors, and there's always another tool to buy and more materials to pay for, plus a day's only got so many hours in it. No, you don't want them for neighbors, just leave 'em alone and let the house do your work for you."

"They'll give up."

"Wouldn't you? They may stick it out longer than most, because he's a man who's got something to prove, but even so he'll call it quits before the house does. Matt, when you write this up—"

"Bare bones," I said.

"Right, and colorblind. Evidence of entry by person or persons unknown. Oh, and make it that the residents just took a quick look-see and couldn't rule out the possibility of theft. In case something does turn up missing, or he decides he wants to report it that way."

*   *   *

I wrote up our report of the incident. Early on, that had become my job.

He started grooming me for it the day he handed me that first ten-dollar bill. His two index fingers picked out the keys and typed up the report, and invited me to read it. It was a straightforward account in serviceable prose, telling how we'd come upon a delivery that was blocking sidewalk traffic at such-and-such a location, and how at our direction the store's proprietor and the deliveryman set about promptly remedying the situation.

Aside from the occasional awkward phrasing, the report's only faults were sins of omission. There was no mention of the twenty dollars, obviously, or of the fact that we left the scene essentially as we'd found it, and that any remedying of the situation would have to wait upon the convenience of the persons involved.

He asked if it looked all right to me, and I said that it did.

"It's a matter of putting in and leaving out," he said. "You say something's a fact, it better be. If you don't want to mention a guy's got a dog, so you don't mention it, and if you get called on it you say you didn't think it was important. Or, what's the word, relevant. But whatever you do, you fucking well don't say it was a cat."

And a few days later, after a relatively uneventful shift, he suggested I take a shot at writing up the report. I had less trouble with the words than with the typewriter—the ribbon needed changing—and I went through our day and wrote up what had come up and how we'd responded. When I was done I read it through once or twice. There was a word I would have changed, but this was before computers, and would have meant retyping the whole page. I decided to wait and see what other changes he'd want me to make.

By the time he'd finished reading, he was nodding his head. "Yeah," he said, "they were right."

Huh?

"Said you were my ticket into plainclothes. 'The kid can write. Get him doing your reports and before you know it you'll be packing your blue bag in mothballs.'"

Did that mean it was all right?

"There's one word here—"

The one I'd wanted to change, and his objection was the same as mine. I don't remember the word or the context, but it made for a sentence that commented on what we saw instead of simply recounting it.

I said I knew what was wrong with it, and how to fix it.

"Other than that," he said, "it's fucking perfect. They're right. You got a gift."

I'd have enjoyed the praise more if I'd thought it was warranted. I said all I'd done was write it up the way it happened.

"That's what everybody does," he said, "or tries to do. And nine times out of ten it winds up sounding like it got messed up on its way through some cop's excuse for a brain. This here, it's the way you talk. I read it and I can hear you talking to me."

"And that's good? Because it just seems to me like the easy way to do it."

"Easy," he said, and rolled his eyes. "You keep taking the easy way out, okay? And start saving up."

For what?

"Suits," he said. "Which you'll need three or four of when your uniform goes in the mothballs."

*　　*　　*

At the time, I took all this with a whole shaker of salt. I was able to see that my reports were better phrased than the ones Vince had been doing, that my sentences were easier to follow and less clunky, but I was trying to satisfy whatever cop wound up reading it, not to get some city editor to give me a byline.

I decided Vince was either all too easily impressed with my writing, or else he was making a show of it so I'd take over a task he found burdensome. But the fact of the matter is I enjoyed the writing I did at each day's end.

Part of what I enjoyed, I'm sure, was knowing I was doing something that had already earned me praise. I'd just been assured that I was good at this, and it's no more than natural to want to do what one's good at.

But it did more than that. Sitting at the typewriter and reporting the events of the previous eight hours was a way of reviewing them and putting them in perspective. I suppose that's a benefit of keeping a diary, something I've never been inclined to do.

The reports had an advantage over writing in a diary, because they were emphatically not for my eyes only. Whether or not a superior officer read them in the ordinary course of things, as soon as I filed a report it became a part of the record, there to be consulted and examined and cited if some other incident linked up with an action or observation of ours.

Say we responded to a domestic, and the battered wife insisted she'd fallen down of her own accord, and the neighbor who'd called it in should mind her own business. You wouldn't believe how often this happened, and we always knew the wife was lying, that she'd fallen because her drunk husband had given her a smack in the mouth, but there was nothing we could do about it. The trick was to write it up in a way that made clear what had happened without spelling it out.

And suppose a week or a month later he hits her again, and maybe he uses something harder than his hand this time, and she winds up in the hospital or the morgue. Any previous complaints? And somebody winds up reviewing our report.

Another element of writing the reports was that of omission. I had to leave out the things we weren't supposed to do. That initial twenty dollars, ten for Mahaffey and ten for me, was not by any means a matter of one and done. There was a lot my partner was prepared to overlook, and a lot of profitable handshakes involved. It was mostly a matter of violations—a blocked loading dock, whatever—but it wasn't impossible to buy your way out of some actual criminal acts. Always non-violent, essentially victimless, but unquestionably an incident where to go by the book was to make an arrest.

"Can we talk this over, Officer?" That was the right way to open the conversation, and those who were savvy enough to know the phrase were halfway home.

Could we talk it over? Sometimes we could, sometimes we couldn't. That was Vince's call to make. If we busted the perpetrator, that of course went in the report. If we talked and he walked, I had some choices. I could report that we'd let him off with a warning, I could say that the lack of evidence had forced us to cut him loose, or, in the absence of any complainants or eyewitnesses, I could leave the entire incident off the books. We'd talk it out, Vince and I, and then I'd work out how to fit words to the tune.

One thing I never did, obviously, was leave open the possibility that money had found its way into our pockets.

* * *

Some did, though.

The first ten dollars wasn't enough to change a man's life, but looked at in a certain way, that's exactly what it did. All it felt like in the moment, I have to say, is that I'd passed a test. Vince and I had already been partners, but the partnership had gone to another level. (I could say we'd become partners in crime, but while that might be technically accurate, it never felt like that.)

There are cops—not many of them, but some—for whom the badge is a license to steal, and that becomes their primary job. They'll respond to calls and make arrests, but that's out of a need to keep up appearances.

And, of course, you never know what'll pay off in the long run. You collar some mope for burglary and you've burnished your record with an arrest, and some months later the burglar's lawyer comes to learn that you've been known to be a reasonable man, and he or his representative has a conversation with you, and in court your testimony is a little shaky, and you fall apart under cross-examination, and the case doesn't even go to the jury. The judge dismisses it, and later you tell the guys in the bar that there's nothing lower on earth than a defense attorney, a prick who trips you up with a whole bunch of words, and everybody assures you that you did everything you could.

And then some.

Vince and I never did anything like that, and had nothing but contempt for the handful of officers who did. We'd never call them on it, or pass the word to the Rat Squad. Blue is blue, after all, and thicker than water. They were still cops but they were crooked cops, and that's not how we saw ourselves.

What were we then, in our own eyes? That's hard to say with certainty, because I found it easy enough to avoid thinking about it much. The extra income made it a whole lot easier to get by on a policeman's salary, especially once Anita and I were married and the babies started coming. First Mike and then Andy, and stuff to buy and new bills to pay, and only one of us working. You could raise a family on a cop's base pay, plenty of people did it, but it was a lot easier if you had a little extra coming in.

I'm not sure exactly how Vince saw it, because our supplementary income was never the subject of a heart-to-heart. We didn't have many of those, long deep conversations where we got into who we really were and how we really saw ourselves and the world. A handful over the years, and always tucked away in a booth at some gin joint where nobody knew us.

Out in Queens one night, Woodside or Sunnyside, after a wake for a fellow officer killed in a line-of-duty shootout. Vince had known him slightly and I'd met him once, and that seemed reason enough to show up but not to linger long. We walked a few blocks, found a bar that looked all right, and settled in to drink whiskey and talk about death.

Other times we talked about women. A week or so before Anita and I stood up at St. Athanasius and said *I do* to each other, I finished typing up my report and asked Vince if he had time for a drink. We walked past our usual place and found a bar that was darker and quieter and less cop-ridden. On our way in, he nodded to a fellow at the bar and got a nod in return.

We sat down and he said, "That guy? I arrested him once. Drunk and disorderly, and he was off the charts on both of those words. I think he did thirty days. What's up, my friend?"

"Day before yesterday," I said, "I was on the phone with Anita, and she asked if I wanted her to come over, and I said I was tired."

"It's like you're married already."

"Well, it was a long shift."

"I remember."

"So I went home, and I was restless, and I got to thinking about one of the doors we knocked on last week."

There'd been an assault on Carroll Street just off Fifth Avenue, a man who'd followed a woman, knocked her down as she was getting the front door open, and was on top of her with his pants open when her screams scared him off. We took her statement and her understandably vague description of her assailant and followed up by going through the building, knocking on doors and hoping somebody had seen something.

"The redhead," Vince said. "Well, auburn, I guess you could call it. I saw her face and I saw yours. What did you do, go back to check if there was something she forgot to tell us?"

That was what I'd have told her, if I'd had to, but when she opened the door she didn't even look surprised to see me. I knew she was married and I knew her husband worked nights, she'd made a point of telling me as much, and the first thing she said once she had the door shut and bolted was, "You got some sense of timing. Ten minutes ago I was touching myself and thinking about you."

I quoted that line to Vince, but all I said beyond that was that I'd spent an hour with her before heading home to Garfield Place.

Vince said there were women who lost interest in you the minute they saw you were a cop. And there were others who were wired the opposite way entirely, and thank God for them.

I said, "I'm getting married in a week. Six days, actually."

"I'll be there."

"Yeah, well, I guess I will, too."

But what did it mean? I was getting married, I loved the woman who was about to become my wife, or at least I thought I did, and we set a date because she missed her period and we figured she was pregnant, but then it turned out she was only late and she told me and said, Well, you're off the hook, and I said No, we were going to get married sooner or later, so this just makes it sooner, and what's wrong with that?

"So?"

So what the hell was I doing on Carroll Street?

His answer waited until we had another round in front of us, and he picked up his glass and gazed into it, as if it held the answer.

Apparently it did. "Getting some," he said. "She made it clear it was there for you, and here's young Matt with just a couple nights left to be a bachelor, and that's how he spent one of them. You have a good time?"

I had, and wasn't that the problem? Otherwise I'd have been able to tell myself I'd just made a mistake I'd never make again, and then perform some nonreligious equivalent of ten Hail Marys on my way to undertaking the role of the faithful husband.

He said, "A week from now, or whatever it is. Six days? You stand there and put the ring on her finger, and it changes things, and you'll find out what changes and what doesn't. And maybe you'll never go to bed with anybody but your wife. That's the way it works for some men, the ring makes that kind of a difference."

I waited.

"Or not," he said. "Or you'll be like most men, and you'll love your wife and the house and the kids and the family dog, the whole package, and you'll do your drinking in bars full of cops like yourself, and the highlight of the evening will be when 'God Bless America' comes upon the jukebox, and everybody stands up and sings along with what's-her-name, the fat girl."

"Kate Smith."

"From sea to shining sea. No, that's the other one, with the fruited plains. That's what you'll do, and you'll steer clear of the singles bars and tell yourself you're comfortable living right, and every once in a while someone'll turn up and you'll look at her and she'll look at you, and the hell with living right and the hell with Kate Smith and the hell with the family dog."

He drank and I drank, and he said, "I'm the last person to tell anyone how to be a husband. I've been living alone for the past four–five years, and the only reason I'm not divorced is my wife's a whole lot more of a Catholic than I ever was. She's got a guy who spends more nights under my roof than I ever did, but once a week she tells some priest about it and does her penance and it's all wiped away, and she can feel good about herself and go home and start working on a new week's worth of sins.

"And whatever works, you know? She gets most of my pay-check to run the house and raise the kids, and it's good I don't have to live on what's left of what the city pays me. And I don't have to fill out any papers or pay a lawyer, and I got one big edge, which is that I can't have a fit of temporary insanity and get married again, because I'm already married.

"So we're on a subject where you'd be crazy to pay any attention to anything I tell you. Will you be a straight-arrow husband? My guess is you won't, but that doesn't have to fuck up your marriage. My catting around didn't help, but there were other factors. I was never home, and most of the time it wasn't because I had somebody else to be with. I didn't come home because home wasn't where I wanted to be.

"Look, it'll be what it is. A week from now, six days from now, I'll be there to watch you take your vows. There's a line in there about forsaking all others, and if you cross your fingers while you say those particular words, who's gonna notice?"

*　　*　　*

I didn't cross my fingers. When the day arrived I stood up there in my navy blue suit, and knocking on a door on Carroll Street, or anywhere else, was the farthest thing from my mind.

I felt a batch of things, and it's hard to sort them out. There was exhilaration—I was getting married, we were starting life as a couple, I could start taking myself seriously as a grown-up, and before I knew it I'd be a father and a homeowner, and how many years would it be before I fell between a couple of subway cars on the way to Canarsie?

Just a thought. One of many, some good, some bad. I didn't dwell on it.

*　　*　　*

We had three days at a resort in the Poconos that billed it-self as the honeymoon capital of the world, a title they earned by furnishing each suite with a heart-shaped bed and a heart-shaped tub, and by limiting their other offerings so that there was nothing to do but stay in your room. Work up a sweat in the heart-shaped bed, then take a dip in the heart-shaped tub.

Rinse and repeat.

On our second night there, I was restless. I slipped out of bed, careful not to wake her, and went downstairs to the cocktail lounge, which was empty except for a couple off to the side who looked as though they'd come to realize they'd just made the biggest mistake of their lives.

The hotel bar featured the predictable line of drinks with cute names—at dinner Anita had ordered something called a Rabbit Habit, and said she liked it but left it unfinished. I'd had a high-ball, bourbon and soda, and now I sat at the bar and ordered bourbon again, this time on the rocks, and I stuck around long enough to have a second and a third.

I don't know what I was wearing, but it was probably the suit I got married in, though I wouldn't have bothered putting on a tie. I hadn't had to go shopping, as I'd already bought the suit and three others a couple of months earlier, right after they'd bumped us up from uniformed to plainclothes officers.

"You need some suits," Mahaffey told me, "and so do I, as far as that goes, and what neither of us needs is to spend a fortune on them." He took me to Robert Hall, their Brooklyn store on Fourth Avenue, and the suits I bought were identical except for color—medium gray, dark gray, dark brown, and navy.

A few years down the line, when they gave me my gold shield, a senior detective from Midtown North took me shopping at Finchley's, on Fifth Avenue in the Forties. He wouldn't let me out of there until I'd sprung for three suits and two sport jackets, and the cheapest of the jackets cost more than I'd paid for all four suits at Robert Hall.

When I'd protested that I already had a closet full of suits, he said he knew I did, and what I did with them was my choice. "Goodwill Industries or the Salvation Army," he said. "Entirely up to you. Matt, you're an NYPD detective, for Christ's sake. You want to look the part."

*   *   *

Getting way ahead of myself here. My mind wanders as one

thought leads to another, and I follow along on the keyboard, dumping my memory onto the computer screen. For a few minutes I was in Pennsylvania, drinking bourbon in the Poconos, and trying not to stare at a pair of newlyweds on the verge of a breakup. Then for a moment I was in Finchley's, picking out the kind of clothes that went well with a gold shield.

Back to the bar, back to the bourbon. I can't remember what I was thinking, but it must have been about what I'd got myself into, and I think the drink was there to dull the edge of thought. Because if I allowed myself, I'd realize it was some mix of anxiety and discontent that had got me dressed and brought me downstairs, and that somewhere inside I was in much the same place as the husband and wife on the other side of the room, stuck at the same little table and unable to look at one another.

The bourbon did its job. It dialed down the volume of my thoughts to where I couldn't hear them.

That's what it does.

And by the time I'd finished the third drink, I was thinking how I'd have to tell Anita about my companions, Mr. and Mrs. Marital Bliss. She'd get a kick out of it. I followed the thought upstairs to our room, and this time I had no trouble falling asleep.

*   *   *

As far as Vince was concerned, it was the way I wrote up our reports that got us out of uniform and into our Robert Hall suits. I always thought he was exaggerating, that nothing I did at a typewriter could have that much effect on two men and their careers. We had some cases that turned out well, and came away from them looking good, and that had to be a factor. And

I was willing to believe that a good report from one or more of my instructors on East Twentieth Street would have made the rounds, leading to my partnership with Vince and following me through it.

And, in fact, the way I put words on paper had something to do with that. There was an exercise they sprang on us where two men stormed into the room while the instructor was in the middle of a sentence. One, wearing jeans and a tee-shirt, was chasing the other, who wore a suit. He caught him and threw him up against a wall, and the guy in the suit moved as if drawing a gun from a shoulder holster, but what he had in his hand was a pen.

And while all of this was going on, a third man entered the room, walked over to the blackboard, picked up one of the erasers, and left the room with it. And then, after the guy in the suit had slapped handcuffs onto the guy in the jeans and led him off and out of sight, the instructor told us what a few of us had begun to suspect.

It was staged, of course, and he called it a test of our powers of observation. He gave us five minutes to write down everything we could remember having seen. What made it difficult, of course, was that for most if not all of the performance, we thought it was real—that the two men were in the room because one was in pursuit of the other, and that one was the good guy and the other the bad guy, and that someone probably ought to intervene, and why was the instructor just standing there? Why didn't he do something?

And, after the reveal, we had to hit Instant Replay and write down what we thought we'd seen. Some of us spent most of our five minutes staring at a blank sheet of paper. My mind had been wandering early on, and the guy in the suit was up against the wall before I'd even noticed something was going on, but I filled in what I remembered with what I figured had to have happened, and I got a lot written, although I missed a lot and got some basic facts dead wrong.

We turned in our papers, and the instructor—his name was Eugene Givens, and it seems to me he held the rank of sergeant—went out into the hall and came back with two men, one in jeans and one in a suit. They were police officers, obviously, and he introduced them, and said we should pay close attention as they reenacted their original performance. And they went out of the room, and Givens picked up a piece of chalk and stood at the blackboard with it, and the door burst open and the playlet was repeated, but this time we all knew we had to pay close attention.

Even so, not everybody spotted the third man, the eraser thief.

Once again, though, we had five minutes to write up what we'd seen, and—well, that's more than anyone needs to know about that particular training exercise. It made its point, and while I certainly didn't think of it at the time, it makes a nice sidebar to Yogi Berra's line. You can observe a lot by watching, but only if you pay attention.

A day or two later we got our papers back, with just enough notes to show that they'd been read, or at least looked at. Before I saw mine, I got to hear it read out loud.

Givens picked three papers for that treatment. He didn't identify the authors, saying there was no need to embarrass anybody, and the first one he read was clumsy and sketchy, and whoever wrote it would have had good reason to feel embarrassed. The second was all subjective—I saw this, I felt that, it was scary when this happened, and so on. You want to leave yourself out of it, he told us. You're a camera, you're a tape recorder, you're reporting what you see and hear and nothing more, because it's not about you.

And then he read what I wrote, my second report, after we knew we were watching a skit staged for our benefit. This, he said, was the way to make a report. It was objective, it was clear, you could read it and you knew exactly what happened, almost as if you were watching it yourself. Of course the guy who wrote it got one or two facts wrong, but that could happen, which was why eyewitness testimony was never as reliable as you hoped it would be, but all the same, this was how a report should be written.

He didn't even glance at me while he was giving me all this anonymous praise. But later, when he cut us loose for our five minute smoke break, he said, just loud enough for me to hear, "Good job, Scudder."

*   *   *

I've thought about this now and then over the years, of course. After I'd left the job and found myself making ends meet by doing as a private citizen some of the things I'd done as a cop, one thing I made very clear was that I was done with keeping track of things and furnishing written reports. I'd act on a client's behalf, I'd do what I could do to bring matters to a satisfactory conclusion, but he wouldn't get a written report or a detailed account of the expenses I'd incurred. I'd sit down with him afterward, and I'd tell him what I had or hadn't learned or accomplished, and I'd come up with a figure of what I felt he owed me, and he could pay it or not.

That basic business plan, if we can call it that, never changed much. At one point I went to the trouble of qualifying for a

Private Investigator's license, and I held it for a while before I gave it back, and during that time I still conducted my business in the same unbusinesslike fashion. No formal reports, no expense accounts. It worked okay.

These days I've been going to my desk just about every morning. I finish my breakfast and sit down at my computer, and the day's first order of business is to spill a little more of my memory into a Word.doc file. That, along with maintaining my sobriety, is each day's workload, and if there are days when it feels like an obligation, it is by and large one I'm grateful to have.

But it's curious now, when I find myself reflecting upon written reports, and how they got me into plainclothes and on my way to a detective's gold shield, even as they were the first thing I cast aside along with that shield.

What keeps happening: I keep thinking about Miss Rudin, my Latin teacher. Every night, working my way through Caesar's *Commentaries*, I was reading one man's matter-of-fact report and finding the English words for it.

It probably wasn't just Miss Rudin, I had a couple of English teachers who played a role in teaching me how to write an English sentence, but I can't shake the feeling that Latin class was the biggest single factor.

I once said as much to Vince Mahaffey, when he was going on about how I'd written our way out of our uniforms. He pointed out that the department was half Irish—probably a low estimate at the time—and that half of them had gone to Catholic school, and wasn't that where they knocked themselves out teaching Latin?

"Except you didn't have to take it," he said. "The ones who

thought they wanted to be priests, they took it. The dumb ones, the ones who wound up on the job, stuck with Shop and Gym. So maybe you got a point."

What I'm writing now is essentially a report, but very different in nature from the ones I wrote at the end of a shift of police work. It's a record of what happened, more or less, but it's neither concise nor direct, and it's not even trying to be objective. *It's not about you,* Gene Givens had told us, but this work is intentionally about me.

That said, I'm just as happy to give the credit to Eleanor Rudin, with an assist to Gaius Julius Caesar. They greased the skids for me when I was an up-and-coming young patrolman, and their influence is still present in the sentences I'm writing now.

Miss Rudin. I never thanked her, I never thanked any of them. I thought of her when I made plainclothes, thought of making the trip to the Bronx and telling her that her teaching had won me a promotion, but it never got any further than a few lines of conversation in my mind.

I remember how her voice broke when she told me and Marcia Ippolito that we wouldn't be able to take third-year Latin. I can see why the school authorities wouldn't greenlight a class with only two students in it, but all the same I've always regretted it.

And would my life be different if I'd taken a third year of Latin? Jesus, look where Caesar got me. If I'd spent a year with Cicero, who knows how far I might have risen? I could have wound up as the fucking Commissioner.

*   *   *

I shouldn't close the book on Vince Mahaffey without

mentioning one other element I learned to leave out of my reports.

I think the term for it is rough justice. I suppose you could classify Vince as a pragmatist, a believer in whatever worked. That showed in the laws he elected not to enforce, the choices he made, like letting a delivery block a sidewalk, that greased the wheels of commerce even as they put a few bucks in our pockets.

He had the same loose approach to going by the book in other areas as well, including those cases where there were no wheels of commerce involved, and no money changing hands. Many of the calls we got were domestics, a term reserved for situations arising among family members, or close associates, or residents of a building. Every patrolman I ever knew dreaded domestics, because they had the least upside—no one ever got a promotion because he calmed down a wife who was trying to stab her husband—along with the greatest possible potential for disaster. Because, whatever you did, she might very well stick a knife in the son of a bitch, and very possibly in you as well.

The ideal outcome in a domestic was to calm things down and restore order without having to make any arrests. Usually at least one of the parties involved was drunk, and if he or she could be induced to sleep it off, it would cease to be a police matter. It might not qualify as a long-term solution, because sooner or later another bottle would lead to another argument, and very likely another call to the precinct. But that would occur on some other evening, and ideally on somebody else's watch.

I was six feet tall, and Vince stood about two inches taller than I, and was broader and heavier. Our size was a definite asset on the job, and this was particularly so in domestics; we looked as though we could handle ourselves physically, and that gave us an edge.

At the time, height was a requirement. They wanted you to be at least 5'8", though the absolute cutoff was 5'7". Around the time I left the force, you started to hear a lot of objections to the requirement. It was seen as discriminatory. Women tended to be shorter than men, and female candidates who would otherwise have been qualified came up, well, short. This was also the case with various ethnic groups—Latinos, Asians. Which was all fine with the faction that would have preferred keeping the NYPD predominantly male and Irish, but it eventually went by the boards.

Which, on balance, was what needed to happen. But it's disingenuous to pretend there isn't a downside, one that shows up when a big wild-eyed drunk who's already had plenty of practice slapping his wife around is confronted by a woman who has to get up on her toes to reach five feet. Yes, she's got a gun she can point at him, but is that what you want?

I don't think Vince ever drew his gun in a domestic, not that I can recall. It was rare enough that it ever left his holster, and I know he never fired it except at the shooting range. Sometimes, when a confrontation was getting tense, he might get ahold of his nightstick, but bare hands were usually all he needed to use.

And sometimes he used them. He'd take hold of a troublesome drunk, push him up against a wall. Swing him around, yank his arm up behind his back. Maybe slap his face. Maybe throw a punch.

Sometimes it went a little further.

One time I remember, a top-floor apartment in a tenement on one of the numbered streets where the Slope and Sunset Park abut one another. A man and a woman, both of them drunk, and this wasn't the first time they'd made enough noise for one of the neighbors to call it in.

We climbed four or five flights of stairs, whatever it was, and that didn't do anything to improve our mood, and neither did the sight of the two of them, him in an undershirt and a pair of boxers, her in some kind of housedress. He was as tall as Vince and must have weighed two-fifty, a lot of it fat, but there had to be some muscle under the flab. She wasn't a whole lot smaller herself, a big woman gone to fat.

From the looks of them, they'd both taken a few slaps and punches. We walked in and found them squared off, staring at each other, and then they were both staring at us.

"You can both get out of here," she said. "Who the fuck invited you, anyway?"

Vince said something designed to cool things down. We'd received a complaint of noise, and we had no choice but to respond to it, and if we could all cooperate we'd nip this problem in the bud. And so on, and it was nothing I hadn't heard him say before, and it usually moved matters toward a peaceful resolution.

But oil on troubled waters held no appeal for these two. The husband started railing at some absent neighbor who he'd decided must have been the complainant, and had a lot to say about just what he would do to him the next time he laid eyes on him, the son of a bitch. And the woman, who had one hand wrapped around a fifth of Calvert Extra, tried to take a drink from what turned out to be an empty bottle.

This was apparently the last straw, and she glanced at the bottle and then at us, and then turned a little to her left and looked at the kitchen sink.

And swung the bottle full force against the sink.

I think they get this from movies. An actor, never the hero, takes hold of a whiskey bottle by the neck and smashes it against a bar or a tabletop, and it's been prepped so that the end breaks off and he's left with a nasty-looking weapon in his hand.

It doesn't work that well in real life, and it didn't work at all well for this particular Jack Elam wannabe. The bottle pretty much exploded, sending shards and fragments everywhere, and she wound up with nothing in her hand but the bottle's disembodied neck.

And she was bleeding. One or more pieces of flying glass had given her lacerations of her hand and arm, and the wounds were superficial but the blood was real, and she stood there in shock, unable to do anything but stare at the blood.

I moved to help her, but she still had a grip on the neck of the bottle, and its jagged end made it a weapon, though not a very useful one. I tried telling her to open her hand and let the thing drop, but the message wasn't getting through, and Vince had also turned toward her and was approaching, looking for a safe way to disarm her, and something made me glance at the husband just in time to see him grab an iron from its perch on an ironing board. He wrapped his big fist around it and snatched it up, and he'd already begun to swing it in a wide arc when I called out my partner's name.

Vince moved, and just in time. The iron didn't miss by much. The momentum cost the husband his balance, and he stumbled forward and might have fallen to the floor, but Vince caught hold of him by the undershirt and straightened him up, and the guy cocked a fist, ready to keep going, and Vince hit him in the chest, a little below the heart, and threw him up against the wall, and followed it up with eight or ten or a dozen body punches, alternating lefts and rights, working that beer barrel of a torso like a heavy bag.

When he stopped, winded, the guy fell to the floor. It was nothing but the wall and the punches that had been keeping him upright. He wasn't unconscious, he hadn't taken any blows to the head, but the fight had gone out of him, along with almost everything else. He was moaning, low-pitched and rhythmically, and I'm not sure he was even aware he was doing it.

I disarmed the woman, which is to say I took the neck of the broken bottle out of her hand and set it aside. She'd quit resisting, and didn't seem to be following what was going on. I sat her down at the kitchen table and took an inch-long sliver of glass out of her arm and looked around for something I could use to clean her wounds.

Vince told me not to bother, that he didn't see anything anywhere, not a dish towel or a piece of clothing, that wouldn't be more likely to cause infection than to do her any good. Cuts like those would close themselves, he said. They weren't the kind of wound you bled to death from.

"Exsanguination," he said, pleased to have found the word. "Like that poor bastard on Prospect Avenue. When was that, March? April?"

It had been sometime in the spring. Neighbors noticed a smell, told the building's super, who let himself in and called it in the minute he saw the body. Young man, late thirties, single, lived alone in an apartment furnished mostly in empty bottles. Worked for years in a Court Street law office, not as a lawyer but as what would now be called a paralegal, although I don't think you heard the term much back then.

They'd let him go, reluctantly, because he was just missing too many days. So there was no employer to notice him not showing up for work, and but for the smell of decomposition he might have spent a month or more on his bathroom floor. That's where they found him, wearing a pajama top but no bottoms. He'd been standing at the toilet, evidently, and he'd lost his balance and fell, and his forehead slammed into the top edge of the porcelain bowl.

That may have been enough to render him unconscious, or the booze he'd been drinking could have done that. Either way, he lay where he'd landed, and the fall opened up a big gash in his scalp, and scalp wounds bleed a lot more abundantly than superficial nicks and scrapes.

So he lay there and bled out. I don't suppose he ever knew what happened to him, any more than if he'd died in his sleep, though no one ever said of bleeding out on the bathroom floor that it was a good way to go.

It happens a lot, actually. I saw a few cases over the years, and drink was always a factor, although God knows you don't have to be drunk to bleed to death from a scalp wound. And there was a prominent actor who died like that, and it's my understanding that he was a drunk. A functioning alcoholic, as they say; he was still getting regular work and fulfilling his obligations, though that didn't do him a lot of good at the end.

*   *   *

When we got out of that top-floor flat, we left nothing but peace and quiet behind us. The wife still sat at the kitchen table, where I'd put her, and you'd have thought she was frozen in place. She didn't speak, didn't move, didn't show any expression, though her eyes were open. I guess she must have been in a blackout, and giving a good impression of a zombie.

Her husband was on the floor where he'd fallen, asleep or passed out. Vince had rolled him onto his side, so that if he vomited he wouldn't choke on it. "If he was gonna puke," he said, "he probably woulda done it by now, but why take the chance?"

"You just saved his life," I said, and he said, "Yeah, I'm a fucking angel of mercy," and we let ourselves out and let the snaplock seal the door behind us. On the way downstairs I said the shift couldn't end soon enough to suit me, and Vince pointed out that we still had two and a half hours to go. We'd been inside that apartment for fifteen minutes tops.

And it was the rest of the evening that got top billing when I wrote it up, because we responded to a call that brought us to the scene of a robbery in progress. Two men, who turned out to be father and son, held up a liquor store, no doubt as an exercise in male bonding. Shots were fired and two people were wounded, one seriously, but ours wasn't the first vehicle to respond. We were too late to hear the gunfire, but right on time to call for the ambulance.

Afterward I drove us back to the stationhouse, and on the way Vince showed me the souvenir he'd taken, an unopened fifth of Old Forester. "The store owner's got enough on his mind," he said. "He's got a bullet in his shoulder, nothing too serious, but his arm-wrestling days may be over. Plus there's the guy he shot, who'll probably recover in time to accept his trophy for

Father of the Year, but maybe not, and all because he couldn't just hand over the money in the register."

"He'd been robbed one time too many."

"So he went for his gun instead, and we had shots fired instead of a peaceful little holdup. Or maybe he saved his own life when he grabbed up that little Smith, because once the guns come out who knows what'll happen? If my grandmother had wheels she coulda been a pushcart."

"But she'd still be your grandmother."

"You're goddam right she would. Old Forester. I was reaching for Old Grand-Dad, which was standing right next to it, and he coulda been a pushcart, too. You think Mr. Bluestone's gonna miss this bottle?"

"He'd want you to have it."

"Or he'd shoot me, but he can't because they took the gun away from him. I'd open this right now if I didn't know better. But it can wait. Just having it's a comfort, you know?"

I knew.

Back at the precinct, I wrote our report. Most of it dealt with the liquor store holdup, but I didn't leave out the husband and wife in the top-floor apartment. In response to another tenant's complaint, we'd arrived to find the apartment unlocked and both parties unresponsive. There'd been a domestic dispute with evidence of some violence, and she bore superficial injuries from a broken bottle, which we'd cleaned, and which didn't appear to require further attention.

And so on.

My memory of the evening is pretty vivid, but I can't be sure of its time slot. It was after I was married, certainly, and after we'd made the move to plainclothes; I can be sure of that because, when I picked up the iron and returned it to the ironing board, Vince said, "Jesus, the bastard could have killed me." And, a moment later: "Or he could have pressed my suit."

It was during the summer, I remember that, and it was probably three or four months after the birth of Michael, my elder son. So we'd still have been living in the apartment we'd moved to after the wedding, just a couple of blocks from Prospect Park. The following summer, when we knew that she was pregnant again, was when we started looking at houses, and thinking about things like decent schools.

I'd bought a three-year-old Pontiac, but almost always walked to and from work unless it was raining. That night we'd been riding around in one of the squad cars, which at the time were mostly black-and-white Plymouth Furies. I filed my report and we got in Vince's car and wound up parked on one of the avenues in front of a shuttered shop that's only name seemed to be the service it offered: FLATS FIXED.

He got out, motioned me behind the wheel, walked around the car and sat where I'd been sitting. He had a good grip on the bottle of Old Forester, and he got the cap off and offered the bottle to me. I didn't often say no to a drink, but something made me shake my head, and he didn't seem surprised. This was before anybody came up with the term *designated driver,* but that was how I saw my role that evening, and evidently so did Vince.

He took a drink, capped the bottle. He said, "Calvert Extra.

That's what they were drinking, wasn't it? That bottle she broke?"

"I guess."

"You see ads for it. 'The Soft Whiskey.' Whatever that's supposed to mean. Maybe they're saying it doesn't burn on the way down. It's like you're drinking colored water, but don't worry, it'll do the job. It doesn't get you drunk, we'll give you your money back."

He took another drink, replaced the cap. He studied the backs of his hands, showed them to me.

"Body shots," he said. "No marks on him, no marks on me. Well, he may be black and blue, but not where it'll show. Hit a man in the face and you can break your hand, plus the effects on him are there for the world to see."

He'd been looking at the bottle, but now he turned his eyes to me. "I lost it," he said. "A fucking iron. He didn't miss me by much, you know."

"I know."

"That kind of situation, hitting him's the right thing to do. You gotta come back at him, and it better be enough so he feels it at the time and still feels it the next day. You follow me?"

I said I did.

"But how much is enough? The old one-two, except it was more like the old one through ten." His hands, closed into loose fists, moved alternately, just a few inches, as if he'd charged them with remembering the punches. "Ten," he said, "or maybe it was twelve. I could've killed the son of a bitch."

"With body punches?"

"When he wound up on the floor, I wanted to kick his teeth in. There was this chair next to him, and my hands wanted to pick it up and break it over his head."

"But you didn't."

"I thought about it."

I said there were lots of things I thought about, and he asked if I was sure I didn't want a drink, because whoever old Mr. Forester was, he made a pretty decent whiskey. "But nothing soft about it," he said. "There's a burn, but I always liked the burn."

I knew what he meant.

"'The Soft Whiskey'," he said, "but there's nothing soft about the empty bottle, and it'd be a pretty good weapon all by itself, but then the silly bitch smashes it and winds up with nothing in her hand but two inches of bottle neck and some broken glass. I'll tell you, our job'd be a whole lot harder if people weren't so fucking stupid."

He had me drive him home, told me to keep the car and pick him up the next day. I let him off in front of his apartment house and waited while he walked to the front door and let himself in. He was carrying the bottle of bourbon, its contents reduced by about half. So he must have put away twelve ounces of bonded bourbon, deliberately replacing the black metal cap after each long drink, but he crossed the broad sidewalk and managed the half dozen stairs without any sign he'd had anything stronger than tap water.

*   *   *

One of the best things Mahaffey taught me was that you could get other people to do what you couldn't do yourself. It was all in how he handled another domestic we caught, and it's in one of the books, pretty much the way it happened.

Briefly, a noise complaint led us to a couple who admitted they may have raised their voices but assured us it wouldn't happen again. No marks on either of them, no signs of a fight, and then we looked a little further and found their little girl, six or seven years old, and the victim of serious physical abuse. Bruises, cigarette burns. Everything you can imagine.

And no case to be made. The kid was scared silent and the parents put up a united front of denial. These days you've got a Special Victims Unit and specialists trained to interrogate juvenile victims, but we had nowhere to go with it.

Mahaffey took a dozen photos of the kid. This was before cell phones, let alone cell phone cameras, but he got hold of a camera and shot a roll of film, and when he picked up the prints we drove into Manhattan and found the bar where the father did his drinking, with his construction crew buddies.

We passed the pictures around, and Vince said, "Look, we're cops. Our hands are tied. But yours aren't." And we got out of there, and they did our work for us, and made a good job of it.

It's in one of the books, I forget which one. In more detail than I've given it here, and recounted pretty much the way it happened.

*   *   *

Vince and I spent a few years in plainclothes before I got the bump up to detective. Sometimes the only difference was what met the eye; instead of the blue bag with the bright gold buttons, we were outfitted by Robert Hall. We might still be in a standard squad car, responding to the same calls and handling them in the same way as when we'd been in uniform.

But sometimes we were in an unmarked car, and sometimes we drew an assignment where it was important we not be instantly recognizable as police officers. Nothing you'd call deep cover, no secret missions to infiltrate a drug deal or a mob heist, but—

Well, here's an example. There was a two-block stretch of Prospect Park West that had a long history as a stroll, which is to say street-level working girls hung out there to solicit customers. Periodically Brooklyn Vice would run an operation that would result in a batch of arrests—and, for a week or two, less pedestrian traffic on the stroll—until things returned to normal.

That was the Vice Squad's job and not ours, and they were welcome to it. But now and then complaints at the precinct level would lead someone to dispatch a couple of plainclothes officers to circulate among the girls and spread the word that calling out to passers-by was a no-no, and you should wait for the John to make an overture. Or that your negotiation with a motorist should be conducted on a side street, not where you were blocking traffic on the avenue. Or that there were certain hours when we were happy to leave you alone, and other hours when we'd collar you just for being there.

And so on.

Once or twice a girl came up with a few bucks, thinking to buy her way out of an arrest that wasn't going to happen anyway. Mahaffey wouldn't take it. "No, that's all right," he'd say gently. "You keep your dough, honey. You're gonna be okay."

And to me, a few minutes later: "What do I want with their money? They work hard for it."

But wouldn't it just go to a pimp?

"Only if they got it to give to him, and they're in trouble if they don't. Ah, Jesus, it's a hard old world. That girl just now? What did she say her name was? Was it Bonnie or Bunny, because it was hard to tell."

I said it could have been either.

"And it's just her street name anyway, so they called her something else ten, fifteen years ago when she was jumping rope and playing jacks. 'A—my name is Annie, my husband's name is Al. We live in Alabama and we sell aardvarks.'"

"Aardvarks?"

"Something with an A. Back in her jump rope days, you figure she said to herself that what she would do with her life was spend it blowing white guys in parked cars? The world's a bastard. Life just happens to people."

*   *   *

Syosset.

If we were going to move out of Brooklyn, I suppose it was as good a place as any. It's about thirty miles away, on the North Shore of Long Island, in Nassau County. Drive time to the city depended on traffic, but you didn't have to drive; the Long Island Rail Road would get you to Penn Station—or to Atlantic and Flatbush Avenues, in Brooklyn.

It was probably a good place for my sons to grow up. The schools were decent.

There were times when I blamed Syosset for the erosion of our marriage—not Syosset specifically, but our having moved away from where we'd been. I'm sure it played a role, but I'm just as sure that the marriage was only following a predetermined route. All the move did was give it a tailwind.

And I suppose the relocation was predictable enough. The way it came about was nothing special. We had a second kid on the way, and our apartment was starting to feel too small. If we had another boy, the two of them could share Mikey's small room—but this was before prenatal ultrasound, and we didn't know what we'd be getting, and my mother-in-law was certain Anita was going to have a girl.

Either way, we felt we could use more room. And it would be nice to have a yard where the kids could play, and where we could do the things families did—grill hot dogs over charcoal briquettes, have a car and a garage to keep it in, and mount a backboard over the garage and shoot baskets. And mow the lawn, and curse the crabgrass. And rake leaves in the fall, and shovel snow in the winter.

And so on.

At the time, there was an NYPD regulation that all members of the department had to reside within the five boroughs of New York. The underlying principle was reasonably sound. The idea was that while you were only working for the city during your hours on the clock, you provided a reserve police presence twenty-four hours a day, seven days a week.

There was an accompanying regulation requiring you to carry your service revolver wherever you went, on or off duty. You might be at D'Agostino's picking up a loaf of bread, with nothing on your mind but the sandwich you were going to make when you got home, but if some kid with a switchblade decided to hold up the cashier, you were there on the spot to blow his head off.

Or something like that.

I'll say this, you got used to it. You'd hear someone say that he felt naked without a gun on his hip, and that wasn't far from the truth, because about the only time you didn't have that gun on your hip was when your clothes were off. That's an exaggeration, you weren't required to carry once you crossed your own threshold, but disarming yourself wasn't always automatic once you got home. I was pretty good about that, before I did much of anything else I'd stow my holstered gun in the top drawer of the highboy dresser, but there were times I'd forget, and I'd be watching television or playing with the boys and realize I was still carrying.

If you invited me over to your house for dinner, I'd show up armed. But what I might do, after a few minutes, was transfer my weapon from its holster to some suitable horizontal surface—a table top, a bookshelf. This was a ritual, with an implicit message: *I'm at ease here, I can let my guard down, it's as if I were in my own home.*

I didn't invent this. I saw other cops do it, and I figured it out, and adopted it myself when the occasion seemed right. It was a choice I might or might not make in a social situation, and it gave me a way of taking my own emotional temperature. If something held me back from disarming myself, well, maybe that was telling me something. Maybe I wasn't quite as comfortable around you as I might have thought I was.

*   *   *

When I gave it all up, the job and everything that went with it, it all took a while to get used to. Going about unarmed was part of it, and not the biggest part; I think I was more conscious of not carrying a badge, of no longer being a law enforcement officer, than I was of not having a holstered gun on my person.

And, of course, not going about armed brought with it, along with a predictable feeling of vulnerability, an offsetting sense of relief. The last time I'd drawn my service revolver I had fired it—with good reason, but certainly with mixed results.

That comes later. I suppose we'll get there, though I can't say I'm looking forward to it.

*   *   *

It was Anita's second pregnancy that got us out of Brooklyn. But the need for an extra bedroom didn't compel us to move all the way out to Nassau County. I was earning a decent salary, logging occasional overtime hours, and, in plainclothes as in uniform, my partner and I continued to draw some undeclared income that the City of New York had nothing to do with. I could have afforded a larger apartment, and my father-in-law had his eye on a house that was coming on the market.

It was in Bensonhurst, on Bay Ridge Avenue, and maybe a five-minute walk from the house he owned. It was a duplex, the property of a friend of George Rembauer's who'd recently sold his home appliances store and was looking to move, as soon as he and his wife made up their minds between Florida and Arizona.

The price would be good, I was assured, and there was a solid and reliable tenant installed in the upper flat, and we'd have the lower to ourselves—a living room, a big kitchen, three bedrooms. Plenty of room for our growing family, and such a convenient location.

The last thing I wanted was to be closer to my in-laws. As it was, we were over there once a week for dinner, a standing date I contrived to miss whenever I could find a pretext. And more often than I'd have preferred I came home to our apartment to find one or both of her parents there—bringing something for Mikey, or some leftover eggplant parm for us.

The two of them never gave me any real reason to dislike them, but I managed fine without one. I found my mother-in-law needy and manipulative, and I just plain didn't care for George. I managed to convince myself, on the basis of no evidence whatsoever, that he knocked his wife around. Something rang a bell, something about the way they were with each other reminded me of various couples Vince and I encountered in Park Slope.

I can't say what it was. George wasn't much of a drinker, and I doubt the police had ever been called to his house. And there were no marks I ever noticed on her face, no bruises, no broken bones. I never asked Anita directly, that can of worms never cried out to be opened, but I steered a conversation or two in that direction.

Once I found a way to tell her about a domestic Vince and I had responded to. "It's remarkable," I said, "how widespread it is. A lot of families look like a cross between *Leave It To Beaver* and *Father Knows Best*, and then you look a little closer and find out the guy's pretty free with his hands."

Nothing. And maybe there was nothing there, maybe he was just what he seemed to be, a solid citizen, an honorable husband and father. Maybe I just wanted to think the worst of him.

I remember one conversation, around the time Michael was born. "You made that promise, right? To bring them up Catholic?"

I had. The priest would have preferred it if I'd converted, but had to be satisfied with the pledge I'd made. George, brought up Lutheran, had done the same. "It's not a big deal," he assured me. "All it meant was she went to St. Athanasius for grammar school. That was fine, it was a good school, and at that age you'd just as soon have them with their own kind. Then we sent her to the public high school, because the last thing me or my Catholic wife wanted was for our kid to get the idea of becoming a nun."

Not likely, I thought.

"But it's all crap," he said. "You don't have to believe it and neither does the kid. You pretend to go along with it, and your kid pretends, and everything works out fine."

That was George, in a rare confidential mood. You know what? On the basis of absolutely no evidence whatsoever, and with no one left alive to say one way or the other, I still think the sonofabitch beat his wife.

*　　*　　*

We got to Syosset by following the road of least resistance.

Herb Polander, a cop a year or two senior to me, had moved there some months ago, and invited us out for Saturday dinner, which he grilled for us in his backyard. He showed us the house, the neighborhood, the school. Before the move, he and his wife and kid had lived with his in-laws in Marine Park, and that remained his official address as far as the NYPD was concerned. "So we still live in Brooklyn," he said, "except we don't. More and more of the guys are doing this, as more and more of the old neighborhoods—well, you know."

Or, as my own father-in-law had put it, you'd just as soon have your kids with their own kind.

The road of least resistance. We never looked anywhere but Syosset. Polander steered me to a real estate agent, who showed us half a dozen houses. They all looked about the same to me, but Anita had a clear favorite, and the agent said he thought a firm offer ten percent below the $50,000 asking price stood a good chance of being accepted. "But don't go with the round figure," he advised. "Ten under is forty-five, but make your offer, oh, $44,693. That way it looks as though you've used some secret formula, and you're not about to budge."

I did as suggested, even though it didn't make much sense to me, and the seller's response was that he'd take forty-five even. I said fine, and that was that.

*   *   *

I could have used the Rembauer house as my official address, but I never really considered it. Instead I went back to my landlady on Garfield Place to see if by any chance my old apartment was available. It wasn't, but she steered me to a friend of hers who had something suitable around the corner on Polhemus.

It was a convenience. I could keep some changes of clothing there, could grab a quick shower on a long hot day, even lie down for a nap. If we wound up working a double shift, I could bed down on Polhemus Place and save myself a commute.

Or if there was something to keep me in town, a game at the Garden, a night on the town with a couple of fellow officers. Or if I was too late to catch that last train, or too drunk to trust myself in expressway traffic.

And if I brought someone home with me, well, that was my business, wasn't it?

* * *

I never did go back and knock on the redhead's door on Carroll Street. Something shifted when Anita and I took our vows, and that kind of lapse looked to be part of the past.

I remember a door Vince and I knocked on together, a woman who'd been on the scene when a hit-and-run driver ran a red light and killed an elderly pedestrian. (The victim, I happen to recall, was 62. Well, that seemed elderly at the time.)

Our witness invited us in, trotted out a plate of cookies, and answered our questions without giving us much that was likely to prove useful. Once we were out of there, Vince said, "I guess you noticed that's there for you if you want it."

Evidently there'd been some verbal cues and significant glances aimed my way, enough to make it clear to my partner that our witness wouldn't mind getting to know me better. It had all sailed right past me.

"The message I get is you're genuinely out of the game," Vince said. "Or you never would have missed it."

I suppose I was, but it turned out that the game was more like football or basketball than baseball. Just because you took yourself out of it didn't mean you couldn't get off the bench and come back in.

* * *

I didn't bring many women to the Polhemus apartment. Four or five over the several years I rented it. Given the choice, I'd opt for her place—but there weren't too many in that category, either. I didn't chase, and I don't think I was compulsive about it, but I suppose I was like that fellow from Tammany Hall. I seen my opportunities and I took 'em.

The first such opportunity came around some months before our move to Syosset. I finished an uneventful shift and wrote up a mostly accurate account of it, and I had a drink with some fellow officers. "I better head home," I told them, and I walked a block or so toward our apartment before I found myself stopping at a bar that looked interesting, where I wound up in conversation with a woman who worked as a legal secretary. It turned out her boss had represented a mope Vince and I had collared for aggravated assault, and she'd been in court when I'd been called to testify.

"After you held up on cross," she said, "we knew we were screwed."

At some point she complained about the jukebox, and I said it would be nice if we could find some place quieter, and she looked pointedly at the fourth finger of my left hand. "Either that's a disguise," she said, "or you're married."

"It's a disguise that fools most people," I said, "but I'm glad you saw right through it."

Did she roll her eyes? Probably. Then she stood up, and I followed her out of there and went home with her. An hour or two later she touched my wedding ring and said, "Oh, well. It's not like it's the first time."

Except it was, for me. But she didn't need to know that.

It's hard to remember how I felt about it. Guilt-ridden? I don't think so. I was aware that I'd crossed a particular line, but all that really seemed to be changed was how I saw myself. Previously I'd been a faithful husband, albeit one whose fidelity had never really been tested, and now I no longer fit that category.

Had I harmed Anita? Not if she didn't know about it, and she certainly wasn't going to hear it from me.

*   *   *

But that was never the point of the apartment on Polhemus, and I don't think I ever brought anyone there more than once. It was, as noted, a convenient place to grab a nap when I had time to kill, and a comfortable place to spend the night when I had reason to avoid the long drive home.

But what got me there almost daily was the need to check my answering machine.

I hadn't foreseen any of that when I took the place. I didn't expect to have a phone installed, let alone a device to answer it and record messages. All of that was a consequence of the shift from uniform to plainclothes, and probably owed a lot to that one assignment we'd pulled, toning down the action on Prospect Park West.

What I learned there, talking with working girls and pimps and other hangers-on, was something a lot of people are born knowing—that people are people. That's not something they teach you at the Academy, nor does it suddenly dawn on you when you start walking around in a blue uniform. On the contrary, you find yourself seeing the human race as composed of two types of people, good guys and bad guys.

In Cop-Speak, citizens and skells.

The uniform reinforced this view. Everywhere you went, the good guys were relieved to see you, while the bad guys avoided eye contact and drifted toward the exits. Good guys and bad guys, citizens and skells. It wasn't all that hard to tell them apart, and you related to them accordingly.

This changed when you left the uniform in the closet and walked around outfitted by Robert Hall. I'm sure I still looked like a cop; that had remained true after I'd turned in my badge and gun, and now, half a century later, some trace of the police officer is evidently there to be seen. Elaine says it's the way I look at people—as though I have a perfect right to look at them, as though it's my job to eyeball them and take their measure. I don't think I do that as much as I once did, but now and then I catch myself at it, so I know it remains a part of how I exist in the world.

Well, you can observe a lot that way, can't you?

In plainclothes, I don't suppose I did any less observing. But I found myself talking to people, and in a way that was less mindful of the distinction between good guys and bad guys, citizens and skells. I noticed the way Vince talked to people on the stroll, the working girls mostly, but also their pimps when we encountered them. Some of them looked the part—oversize purple hats, dark or mirrored sunglasses, suits from Phil Kronfeld's, long low convertibles that were mostly tailfin—but not all of them ran that strongly to type. The common denominator was race; they were all what Mahaffey might call Norwegians.

The ones I encountered, that is, although I came to learn that pimping wasn't exclusively an African-American occupation. There were white pimps, and from more than one source I heard of a fully observant Hasidic Jew from Borough Park, with side locks and a full beard and the black hat and all, who had half a dozen girls working out of a house on Avenue M in Midwood. If he didn't exist, he at the very least starred in an enduring urban legend.

What I got to know—which I suppose anybody with an open mind could have figured out faster than I did—was that working girls were people, too, and so were the men who ran them, and the men who paid them for their services. They were all just playing the cards they'd been dealt, living the lives they'd been handed, and, well, doing the best they could.

And what else, really, does anybody do? I don't know how many AA meetings I've been to, but the number's certainly a high one, and I've heard a great many people tell their stories. A lot of them have had things to say about their parents, and a lot of those parents would seem ill-suited to their roles. Stunning neglect, appalling mental and physical and sexual abuse, on and on and on.

But the conclusion, almost invariably, has been that Daddy did the best he could. Or Mommy, or both of them. And this almost tautological business of having done one's best can't be reserved exclusively for parents.

So we're all of us doing the very best we can?

Outlier examples are hard to swallow. That cop in Minneapolis, with his knee on a man's neck, was he doing his best? Did Ted Bundy do his best? Did Hitler?

Maybe. Maybe it's just a definition of the universal human condition, maybe whatever one does, however heinous, is the best one could do with what one has been given.

Or not. What do I know? I never got to take third-year Latin.

*   *   *

The point was I started talking to people on the street, hookers and pimps and other hangers-on. I let them know that my interests were far-ranging, and that they could possibly do themselves some good by sharing information with me.

In other words, I was lining up sources. Snitches, if you will. Vince, who'd been working the same Brooklyn streets for most of his career, already had a fair number of people in the neighborhood who'd feed him information, and I was building on the example he'd set me.

Nothing happened for a while, and I figured I was wasting my time, albeit in an interesting fashion. And then one day a very low-level pot dealer gave me the side eye and said, "You didn't hear this from me, right?" and went on to pin a name on the unidentified shooter who'd stepped up next to a gray Buick Riviera waiting for a light at the corner of Sixth Street and Seventh Avenue to turn from red to green. With two witnesses at the scene, he'd fired three bullets into the head and chest of the unaccompanied driver and scurried across the street to where another car was waiting for him.

Black man, dark clothes, average height, average weight. That was all the two witnesses could come up with, and all they knew about the getaway car was it had four tires. The victim was of Portuguese descent, born in the Azores, owned a laundry and dry cleaners half a mile from the crime scene, lived above the store. No arrest record, nothing on his sheet but parking tickets, and none of his neighbors had anything to say about him, beyond the one woman who complained that his shop reeked of the cheap cigars he smoked.

We didn't get the case, a couple of uniforms were first on the scene and a couple of detectives from our precinct picked it up, only to have it taken away from them by Brooklyn Homicide when nothing led anywhere. The victim's life looked blameless, his marriage appeared to be solid, and no one had any reason to call him a nasty name, let alone blow his brains out.

"Wrong guy," my snitch said. "Wrong Buick Riviera. Guy burned two people bad in a coke deal, but it was a different guy in a different car. Fool shot the wrong man, and now he wants to get paid, but who's gonna pay him for shooting the wrong man? He out there looking for the right man to shoot, but that man, he most likely drove *his* Buick Riviera clear to Georgia by now."

And that's as much as I remember, and way more than anybody needs to know, about that particular case. I passed on what I'd learned, but not where I'd learned it, to one of the original detectives, who handed it on to the appropriate detective at Brooklyn Homicide. It was, everybody agreed, the kind of case that could only be solved this way, with someone ratting out the perpetrator, because no other connection existed between Senhor Oliveira and the man who killed him, who were both doing their best.

* * *

Along with the shooter's name and motive, my snitch passed along the address where he could most likely be found, and enough information about the driver of the getaway vehicle so that both men were soon in custody. The shooter hadn't gotten rid of the murder weapon—he figured it would be useful when he got a chance to shoot the right person, thus completing the assignment and assuring he'd get paid.

Right. Meanwhile, his accomplice took a look at the tea leaves and went for a plea, and turned up in court to testify against the shooter, who wound up having an audible argument with his lawyer. "Tell 'em I made an honest mistake! I shot the wrong person!"

It was a strategy his attorney declined to pursue, but it made the tabloids and the local news, and that was enough to inspire the lawyer to request a mistrial. Fat chance. The jury wasn't out long enough to order sandwiches, and the sentence was life without parole. If he's still alive, he's probably still inside.

* * *

Funny thing. The defense he argued for, the honest mistake argument, worked once. In the Old West, as I heard it told, and back in the late nineteenth century. One man was in a hotel room with a prostitute when another man kicked in the door and came in with two guns, blazing away until both were empty. He missed his intended victim but killed the woman, and he was subsequently arrested and charged with her murder.

He swore he hadn't meant to kill her, that he didn't even know her and had nothing against her. And the judge agreed that murder implied intention, and the defendant had clearly held no intention of inflicting harm of any sort upon the victim. He'd set out to murder her companion, but had failed altogether in that attempt, and thus the only crime he'd committed consisted of breaking down a door, and the prosecution had neglected to level that charge against him. Not guilty, case closed. Next!

I can't swear that it ever happened, and it does sound too good to be true. Still, it makes its point.

*　　*　　*

I'd described my tip as having come from a local source my partner and I had jointly developed, and Vince and I both wound up with a commendation in our files. Vince was grateful for this, but told me it was really all my doing. "I never paid much attention to that mope," he said. "Always there, and what he was selling was mostly seeds and stems, and he must have been his own best customer, because I never saw him that he wasn't stoned. Even if something went down right in front of him, you wouldn't expect him to notice."

I said I thought my snitch was probably high all the time, but maybe not as high as he let you think.

"There's drunks like that," Vince allowed.

And anyway, he hadn't seen anything, hadn't left the corner or been anywhere near the site of the shooting. He'd received a report from a woman he knew, who also happened to be a woman the shooter knew.

"Biblically," I said, "in both instances. She was our guy's

girlfriend, and then the other guy made a move on her, and all our guy wound up with was a resentment."

What I wound up with, along with the commendation, was a strong belief in the value of cultivating sources. Because you really never knew who might find out something useful and pass it along to you. So I found myself spending more and more of my time in places where the people I encountered had the potential of telling me something I'd be glad to know.

If I'd been an investigator for the Securities and Exchange Commission, I suppose I'd have found those likely snitches in banks and brokerage houses and board rooms, and they might have been every bit as interesting as all my hookers and shoplifters and drunks and junkies.

But maybe not.

It had never been unusual for me to stop somewhere for a drink once I was off the clock, and increasingly I took to seeking out bars that were on the shady side, and spending more time in them. Two hours some nights. Or three, or more.

A lot of hours I might have spent with my wife and young son, and spent instead with, well, shady people.

I told myself it was work, and it was. I couldn't put in for overtime, or get reimbursed for the dollars I laid down on bar tops, but I was receiving genuine value for my money. At best I was forging relationships and picking up information, but at the very least I was having a couple of drinks, and that never failed to seem like a good idea.

And where would I have been otherwise? Home?

If you'd asked me, and if you'd picked a time when I felt like talking, I'd have told you I was happy with my wife and glad to be married. I might have pulled out my wallet and shown you a picture of my son.

And that was true enough. The whole truth? No, hardly that. But true enough.

So why was it taking me so long to get home from work? Because I was devoting those hours to becoming a little bit better at my job. And wasn't that to everyone's benefit?

*   *   *

The machine that answered my phone on Polhemus Place would seem impossibly primitive in today's world of voice mail. It would play my outgoing message: "Hi, I'm not here to take your call. Leave your name and number at the tone and I'll get back to you." Then there'd be a tone, and it would record whatever the caller said in the next five minutes or so.

If I wanted to listen to a message, I had to be there in person to press the appropriate button, and after I'd played the message I could keep it or erase it. There may already have been machines that allowed you to access your messages remotely, and that would have been handy, but that wasn't the kind I had.

And any answering machine at all was apt to surprise a fair number of the people who reached it. Early on, most of my callers rang off without leaving messages, though some stayed on the line after the tone, waiting a minute or two for something to happen.

One time I made what was supposed to be a quick stop on my way home to Syosset, only to discover that my entire message tape was full. It was all the work of one woman, and she was desperate to reach her sister in Maspeth, but she kept getting my number, probably because she kept dialing it, and her patience waned even as her frustration mounted. "You keep saying you're not there to take my call. If you're really not there then why do you keep picking up the phone?" and "I know this is the right number, you stupid son of a bitch! I've been dialing this number all my life. Why are you answering the wrong number? What's the matter with you?"

And so on.

The handful of people who called me intentionally got the number from one of the business cards I'd handed out. I'd had a job printer a few blocks from the stationhouse run off a batch of one or two hundred, whatever the minimum was, and the text was equally minimal: Three lines—my first and last name, my new phone number, and LEAVE MESSAGE.

I got the idea of handing out cards from the Brooklyn Homicide detective who'd given me one of his. I don't think I ever found a reason to call him, but he was the first cop I knew who had a business card, and I was impressed, and by the time we made the move to Syosset, I had worked out how everything could fit together, business cards and an apartment and a telephone and a machine to answer it.

These days just about everybody over the age of ten has a phone in his pocket, and every new patrolman picks out one of a dozen designer templates and orders a few hundred business cards from whatever cop shop supplied the rest of his gear.

For me, the cards were a good move even if nobody ever dialed the number. A lot of my conversations on street corners and in saloons worked their way around to invitations to let me know if anything came to mind, or if there was some confidential information they wanted to pass on. My card was something they could take away from the conversation, something tangible that would bring the moment back to mind when it surfaced the next day in a purse or pocket.

And now and then there'd be a message:

"Uh, this here's Billy at the parking lot. If you get a chance."

Or

"Not saying who this is, but somebody should take a look at Roger McAlpin for that thing on Seventh Street. That's Tall Roger, Roger that limps, you know who I mean."

Like that.

* * *

It was sometime during the first year in Syosset that someone suggested I think about the Sergeants Exam. It was a way to move up in the Department, and the higher rank brought a higher salary. As a police officer, you were represented by the Patrolmen's Benevolent Association; sergeants had their own union, called not surprisingly the Sergeants Benevolent Association, and it may have had a little more clout than the PBA.

At first I thought the whole thing was out of reach for me, but then I had a look at a few pages of sample questions, and I figured it was a test I could pass. There were things you had to know, which would entail a few weeks of study, but it seemed to me that a majority of the questions were the sort they asked you in high school reading comprehension tests. If you could read a fairly complex paragraph and make sense out of what you'd read, the City of New York was ready to hand you the keys to the precinct house, or at least give you a seat at the front desk.

I told Vince I was thinking about it. "Bill Walsh says I should take it," I said, "and the sooner the better. He's got the flash cards he used when he was studying for it, and he says I can borrow them."

Walsh was a desk sergeant at the Seven-Eight, and more approachable than most. Vince said, "Flash cards."

"He said they were helpful."

"I looked at the questions once. Not that I thought I could be a sergeant, not that I even wanted to, but out of curiosity. I got a headache reading them."

I knew what he meant. One question that didn't have any obvious connection to police work presented you with a batch of facts: *Susan is older than Mark but younger than Rita. Five years ago, Mark was one and a half times Shirley's age. Rita's younger brother is a year older than Shirley's sister—*

"You could pass it," Vince said.

"I don't know."

"Yeah, you've got the mind for it. You could take the questions apart and figure them out. And the hard facts, the stuff you have to study for, you and Anita could run those flash cards until you were letter-perfect. You'd have to put in the work, but that's the thing. You'd do it, you'd take your best shot, you'd put your ass in the chair and get the work done."

"Maybe."

"And then what?"

He'd lost me.

"You pass the test," he said, "and probably with flying colors. That qualifies you to be a sergeant, and you're on the list when an opening comes up. 'Officer Scudder, there's a sergeant's slot open at the One-Two-Two.' That's right on Hylan Boulevard in Staten Island, and don't ask me how I remember the address. 'It's yours if you want it, Officer Scudder, or you can wait for something to open up in the ass end of Queens.'"

"I don't think—"

He waved away whatever I was going to say. "Where they wind up putting you is pretty much beside the point, Matt. It's easier or harder to get to from Syosset, that's all, and it's probably temporary anyway, because they'll move you again a few years down the line when you sit the Lieutenants Exam. Because that's what all of this is about, isn't it? Making something of yourself, moving up in rank."

"You think it's a bad idea?"

"I think it's the way a cop gets ahead. You like Bill Walsh?"

I said I liked him well enough. I didn't know him all that well, but he'd always struck me as one of the good guys.

"You want to *be* Bill Walsh? Come in every morning, sit at his desk, do what he does?"

I'd never really thought about it.

"What you and I do," he said, "is walk around and drive around and knock on doors and sometimes kick 'em in. We go around being cops. What the sergeants and the loos and the captains do is see to it that we do our jobs right. You take the sergeants exam, you're on track to stop being a cop and start being a boss of cops. That's important, take away the department's organization and administration and we're all of us cut off at the knees."

He kept talking, but I wasn't taking it in. Instead I was imagining myself in a role very different from the one I'd been playing, an essentially administrative role. I wouldn't be walking a stroll alongside Prospect Park, handing out my minimalist business cards to whores and pimps and junkies and unclassifiable mopes.

No, I'd be making peace between partnered patrolmen who'd begun rubbing each other the wrong way, and fielding citizen complaints of overzealous meter maids, and adjusting schedules so that this officer could get a morning off to go to a funeral and that one could get to a wedding in Yonkers.

"And you reach a point," I heard Vince say, "when what it's mostly about is asses."

Huh?

"Which ones to kick," he said, "and which ones to kiss."

Politics. I hadn't even thought about that aspect of it, but of course that would become an element. Getting along by going along. Playing the game.

I said I didn't want any of that. I just wanted to be a cop and keep on doing what I was doing. Next time somebody asked me about the Sergeants Exam, I'd say I wasn't interested.

He shook his head. "What you say," he said, "is that you'll be able to get down to studying for it when things ease up a little at home. You don't want to sound like a man who lacks ambition."

"Even if that's what I am?"

"That's not what it says on your business cards."

"All it says—"

"What it says is here's a man spending his off hours lining up snitches so he can crack cases that don't even exist yet. What's that if it's not ambition?"

"Maybe I just don't want to go home."

"There's easier ways to stay out of the house. You're out on Long Fucking Island, you could spend every free minute on a golf course and half your working hours talking about it."

"Like Simmons," I said, naming a cop we both knew who wanted to be Sam Snead.

"What was that he said the other day? 'So I whipped out my niblick.'"

"Sounds like indecent exposure."

"Jesus, it does at that. Matt, you got an ambition, whether you know it or not. You want to be a detective. Don't tell me you haven't thought about it."

"I've thought about it."

"Of course you have. You're a patrolman, you bump into something that turns out to be interesting or important or complicated, next thing you know some clown with a gold shield takes the case away from you. 'Thank you very much, Officer, and we'll let you know how it all works out.' That doesn't have to happen too many times before you start wanting to be the clown with the gold shield."

I said I didn't know how to make that happen. He said what I already knew, that there was no exam to take, no application to fill out.

"What you do," he said, "is what you been doing. You don't have to press any harder than you've been pressing."

"Okay."

"And keep your nose clean. The commendations in your file can get offset in a hurry by anything negative. Put in your time in the bars and on the street corners, but walk away before the shit hits the fan. You're a man who likes a drink."

"Not when I'm on the clock."

"Never?"

Maybe once or twice. But Vince himself—

"I ain't going nowhere," he said. "I'm a veteran patrolman finishing out my twenty, and I'm not on a fast track or even a slow track, and if every once in a while I take a drink, nobody feels the need to call attention. For you, not so much as a glass of beer while you're on duty."

"Okay."

"And don't go over the line even when you're not. My personal opinion, you haven't got a problem. I've seen you make your load plenty of times, and I haven't seen you stagger or talk too loud or tell the same story over and over."

"Jesus, I hope not."

"But if I was to worry, it'd be about that long drive home to Whatchacallit."

"Syosset."

"Breezing along on the LIE, trying to make time. How many times you been pulled over?"

"There's no record of it."

"Once? Twice?"

"Twice, both times for having a heavy foot."

"Speeding."

"Once I was close to fifteen miles over the limit. The other time I wasn't doing more than keeping up with traffic, but I guess the guy had a quota to make."

"And both times you showed your badge and apologized for being over the limit, and professional courtesy carried the day. Is that about right?"

It was. Being a law enforcement officer had certain side benefits, and one was a general dispensation from traffic laws. That was a long time ago, but I don't imagine it's changed much. If the guy who ran the stop sign turned out to be your fellow officer, were you going to write him up for it? No, probably not.

"If you'd hit something," Vince said, "like anything at all, there'd all of a sudden be a gap in the solid blue line, because whoever showed up would have no choice. Even if some asshole was going westbound in the eastbound lane and smacked into you from out of nowhere, somebody'd have to cover his own ass by giving you a field sobriety test. And you'd flunk it."

So. Don't go over the speed limit, or break any traffic laws, because there was always the chance you'd run into the rare bird who didn't buy the idea of cops looking out for their brother officers, and who maybe had a hard-on for the NYPD and New Yorkers in general. And a few other things to look out for—and, most important, if you'd drunk enough to feel it, don't drive anywhere. If you absolutely had to get home, take a train. Otherwise, spare yourself an uncertain hour behind the wheel and sleep it off in your apartment.

Because wasn't that the real reason you paid the rent each month? You didn't need a machine answering your phone, you could pretend you were an actor and get yourself an answering service. And most of the women you were likely to walk out with had their own place, and in an emergency you could always find a hot-sheets hotel.

But if you wanted to sleep off a drunk, you really needed somewhere to lie down.

*   *   *

It was good advice, and I recognized it as such the minute I heard it. And I took it to heart, and I followed it.

Mostly.

Not a hundred percent, because it's hard to be a hundred percent of anything once there's whiskey in the jar. First the man takes a drink, as one hears it said, and then the drink takes a drink. And even if that's where it stops, before the third step of *and then the drink takes the man,* it's way too easy for something to go wrong.

Sometimes you forget what you're supposed to do. Sometimes you remember, and decide to make an exception. Just this once you'll make a night of it. Just this once you'll drive home even if you know better.

Just this once.

I got away with it. I got pulled over three more times that I remember, once in my own precinct in Brooklyn, twice on the Long Island Expressway. In the Seven-Eight, the fellow who stopped me apologized for not having recognized my car; on the LIE, professional courtesy let me skate both times, no problem, you have a good night now.

And one night there was a fender-bender on an access road, another poor son of a bitch who was at least as drunk as I was. He thought the accident was all his fault, when in fact it was probably about sixty percent mine. I identified myself as a police officer, and he thought I was about to arrest him. We established that damage to both cars was minimal, and the important thing was to find a rug that we could sweep the whole thing under.

So he went his way and I went mine. No harm, no foul.

That episode of Bumper Cars got my attention. The other

incidents might have put my hopes for a gold shield in jeopardy, but breaking a perfectly arbitrary speed limit wasn't necessarily unsafe, and I could make the same argument for driving with an elevated blood-alcohol level. Just numbers, and they might get me in trouble, but what real harm was I doing?

But this time I'd hit a car. I didn't hurt it much, my own car came out of it worse than his, and neither of us wound up with a scratch, so if you were going to have a collision this was the kind to have.

And I guess I learned from it. I won't contend that I never drove drunk after that, but I never got in another accident or attracted the attention of another traffic cop—at least not until after I got bumped up to detective, at which point I figured I could take the whole business a little easier.

Because what you did behind the wheel might stand in the way of a promotion, but it wouldn't countermand it. Once they gave you that shield, you'd have to do a lot to make them take it away.

So you could say I was lucky.

* * *

Lucky.

Today's my birthday. September 7, 2022. That's ten or eleven weeks after I started writing whatever this is, and an even eighty-four years after I was born. Elaine asked me what I'd like for a birthday breakfast, and I suggested we make an occasion of it and go across the street to the Morning Star. We sat at an outside table. She ordered French toast and I ordered blueberry pancakes and we shared the two dishes, along with orange juice and coffee. She makes better French toast than the cook at the Morning Star, and better pancakes, although the blueberries were a nice touch. The sun was out but the air was still comfortably cool, with a light breeze blowing in off the Hudson. If it wasn't a perfect morning, it wasn't off by much.

Then we came home and I sat down at the computer and read what I wrote yesterday, which is how I generally get started. And I read the last sentence, *So you could say I was lucky,* and thought about it for a while.

And hit the return key twice, and wrote: *Lucky.*

And that's where I am.

It is pointless, I sometimes tell myself, to wonder about what might have happened—because it didn't, did it? What actually did happen, the great stream of yesterdays that resolved themselves into today, now bear an appearance of inevitability. Whether or not one's destiny was written in the stars, the present reality is indelibly written in the here and now.

Pointless to echo John Greenleaf Whittier, the poet:

> For all sad words of tongue and pen,
> The saddest are these: "It might have been."

I had to Google it to get the words just right and make sure who wrote them, but they'd stayed with me since high school English. I wound up reading the whole poem again, over a hundred lines of bouncy rhymed couplets. Boy encounters girl, and each has secret thoughts about the other, and they go their separate ways forever, but neither of them really gets over it. It has the feel of doggerel now, and maybe it always did, but I was a less critical reader seventy years ago.

In its day, I learned, the poem was enough of a success to inspire a response from Bret Harte, whose name I know although I don't believe I've ever read any of his work. But I just now read his parody, an echo of Whittier's original, in which boy gets girl, to their profound and enduring mutual disappointment:

> If, of all words of tongue and pen,
> The saddest are, "It might have been,"
> More sad are these we daily see:
> "It is, but hadn't ought to be."

How does an old man get through the days? I'll tell you, it's not that hard, not with Google and Wikipedia, not with a cyberworld so quick to branch off into so many paths, all of them leading in different directions.

*   *   *

Still thinking about luck.

It's not uncommon, in AA meetings, for someone to speculate on what might have been had he gotten sober earlier. Gifted with a little more perception and little less denial, isn't it possible things could have turned out differently?

A couple of years ago, when perception edged out denial on a rather different field of battle, I went to an audiologist and learned, to neither her astonishment nor my own, that I needed hearing aids. Before I left, I speculated that I probably could have used them a couple of years earlier.

"Ten," she said, and went on to tell me that was how long it took on average for age-related deafness to prompt a person to do something about it.

That struck me as an uncommonly long time to spend asking people to speak up, but it was probably ten years earlier, or close to it, when ambient noise started to be a problem. There were certain restaurants where other people's conversations drowned out one's own. Dialogue was hard to catch in some movies and TV shows, especially British imports.

Ten years. And how much sooner might I have been well advised to put the plug in the jug and swap the barstool for a folding chair in a church basement?

Say what? Speak up, will you? It's hard to hear with all this noise.

* * *

Back again.

Something kept me away from my desk for a few days. It's been a week since I turned 84. Last night Elaine and I went downtown for dinner with Ray Gruliow at the latest incarnation of a restaurant a few doors down Commerce Street from his house.

Ray had stayed active as a defense attorney longer than Elaine or I had clung to our respective careers, but he's been retired for a while now—although once in a while a colleague will drop by for a consultation. "I think it's to impress the client," he said. "'Hard-Way Ray suggested' sounds authoritative, doesn't it? And I get paid a few dollars for my wisdom, which is probably more than it's worth."

It was just the three of us. I can't remember when his most recent marriage ended, or the name of his most recent wife. We lingered at table longer than one usually does at an alcohol-free dinner, and at one point he labeled himself as being between marriages, which was a phrase Elaine and I recalled on our way home.

"First of all," she said, "shouldn't it be *among* marriages? Given that we're talking about more than two?"

I said she might have pointed that out, as almost everyone enjoys having his grammar corrected.

"I think it's diction, not grammar. Anyway, I didn't think of it until just now. And he used the right word after all, because he's between his most recent marriage and his next one. I was just being snotty."

"Okay."

"And I'm not sure what he was being. 'Between marriages.' He's not seeing anyone, is he?"

"If he were, he'd have brought her along."

"If it was even close to serious."

"Or even if it wasn't."

"To show her off. You're right. I guess he was being ironic, and why can't I leave it alone?"

"You're worried about him."

"He didn't look good, did he? And once or twice he seemed to drop a stitch. He caught it and covered it, but still."

He's older than I am, though only by a couple of years. We're both of us old enough, and see each other infrequently enough, to wonder on parting if we'll see each other again. Or if, by the time we do, one of us will have forgotten who the other is.

There they are again, McGuinness and McCarty.

Elaine knew Ray before I did, although I'm not sure he's aware of it. He was, on one or two occasions, a client of hers, which is to say that he spent some time in her bed and left some money on her nightstand. She told me as much when Ray became a principal in a case I was working, and by the time it had resolved, he and I had become close.

Did he recognize Elaine when he met her? I don't know. Nobody ever said anything. And what did it matter?

Ah, Jesus.

Well, it got me to my desk this morning. I think I let myself get mired in a world of *What If*, wondering whether it was in fact good luck or bad that let me get away with driving drunk. What difference does it make? What happened is what happened.

So this entry and the one before it will be something to cut at some future date. For now I'll just get on with it.

But not today.

*   *   *

For a while there, the gold shield was my green elephant.

My father, when I was nine, ten, maybe eleven years old: "How'd you like to make ten dollars, Mattie? You can do it without saying a word or moving a muscle. All you have to do is spend the next ten minutes without thinking once of a green elephant."

I guess nowadays they'd call that a Dad joke. I was young enough to make an effort, and of course I couldn't manage it, because to try not to think of something is perforce to be able to think of little else. I gave my mind things to do, I ran through the Yankees batting order and the seven-times table, and, through it all, there was that fucking elephant, now forest green, now lime green, swinging its trunk and flapping its ears . . .

"Now isn't that something? I bet you never once in your life thought of a green elephant, and now you can't think of anything else."

I got the point, and it evidently stayed with me. But did I get the ten dollars? I recall the incident vividly, but I somehow remember it with two irreconcilably different endings. In one: "You know what? You gave it your best shot, and nobody could have done any better. Here you go." In the other: "You know what? This here is going right back in my wallet, but the lesson you just learned about the way the mind works, that's going to be worth lots more than ten dollars."

I remember it both ways, and I'm not sure either of them ever happened. Maybe there was no ending. Maybe he just patted me on the shoulder and went around the corner to get himself a beer, and maybe my mind dreamed up both endings and gave them equal time, but together they add up to another lesson, right up there with the green elephant—a lesson about memory, and just how reliable it is.

I always knew that about eyewitness testimony, had it drummed into me at the Academy, confirmed it on the job. But it's something you figure only really applies to other people.

The green elephant.

I'd had occasional thoughts of becoming a detective ever since I got used to seeing the ones at the Seven-Eight. They were all senior to me, as one would expect, and there was an air of self-confidence and proficiency about them that made them enviable even as it put them out of reach.

When I took the apartment on Polhemus Place, when I installed the answering machine and ordered the business cards, I was willing myself not to think of the green elephant even as I was standing there with a peanut in my hand, trying to tempt the beast. It seemed to me that the best way to become a detective was to distinguish oneself as a plainclothes police officer.

Looking back, I'm not sure that's true. There are a number of ways to play departmental politics, and sometimes they work. But I didn't have the instincts or the inclination for the game. Or the time—I was busy being a cop.

And it was working. I was developing a circle of sources, mostly but not exclusively in my home precinct. The work was paying off, and then Vince and I broke a case, and while it wasn't exactly the French Connection, a lot of heroin was confiscated and a lot of arrests made—and, after the DA's office did a little of the usual log-rolling and horse trading, a couple of bad guys wound up doing serious time at Green Haven. That put commendations in both our files, and some public ink to go with it; while the press focused on the detectives we handed off to, Vince and I did get our names in the paper.

Then I killed a man, and that tipped the scales.

If you were going to shoot someone, it would be hard to find a more suitable man than Rufe Taggart. He was from somewhere in West Virginia, and according to one newspaper account his mother could have been in the DAR; she'd had an ancestor who'd fought in Washington's army at the Battle of Trenton.

He was 37 when we came into each other's lives, and he'd spent a dozen of those years in one prison or another, and killed two people that we knew about. One case fell apart when a witness disappeared—dead or in the wind, depending which rumor you believed. The other got plea-bargained down to manslaughter.

I suppose he was a career criminal, although his wasn't much of a career. He made ends meet with snatch-and-grab burglaries, and muggings that were the adult equivalent of taking a smaller kid's lunch money. These ventures served to support his real passion, which was sexual predation. They didn't start the Sex Offenders Registry until 1996, and by then he'd been dead for thirty years, but if the timing had worked out he could have been a charter member. He started with window peeping in his teens and did a little of this and a little of that, all on his way to discovering what really did it for him, which was forcible sexual relations with minors.

Rufe liked kids—or hated them, as you prefer. He didn't seem to care if they were black or white, male or female, which is relatively uncommon; sexual predators usually fixate on their own race, and confine themselves to the same or the opposite sex. I've since heard an offender described as an equal-opportunity pervert, and, all these years later, the phrase brought Rufe to mind.

Mahaffey and I were about halfway through an evening shift,

wearing our Robert Hall suits but driving around in a black and white squad car, when the radio let us know about an apparent crime in progress—screams and gunshots coming from a ground-floor apartment at an address just two blocks from us. Vince called in that we'd take it, and I got us there and we left the car double-parked. A woman was in front of the building, and she pointed us in the right direction.

It was an abandoned building, she told us, but there were squatters in some of the apartments. We went in with guns drawn. I'd never discharged my revolver except at the firing range, and aside from infrequent cleanings I couldn't remember the last time it had left its holster. But I had it in my hand, and it was a good thing that I did, because the first thing I saw was a man pointing a gun at me.

He pulled the trigger and my first thought was that I'd been shot, even though I hadn't felt anything. But I hadn't heard anything, either, because the pistol he was firing had jammed. He said something—"Shit," probably—and threw the gun down, and I suppose his next move would have been to raise his hands and surrender, but the message that he was no longer a threat hadn't yet made it to my brain. I'd been in the process of returning fire, and I went on with it, and I didn't miss.

My shot, I learned later, could not have been improved upon, and luck, I've always known, had more to do with it than marksmanship. I don't recall taking aim, just pointing, and the pull on the trigger came of its own accord. The round I fired took him in the heart and death must have been instantaneous, or close to it. For an instant or so, while the report of the gunshot bounced off the kitchen walls, I thought Vince must have fired it. Then the message got through that I was the shooter, and that the man I'd shot was dead.

I guess I was in a state of shock. Vince got hold of me, took the gun out of my hand, returned it to my holster, grabbed a chair, got me seated on it, and kept up a stream of conversation, telling me I'd saved both of our lives, I'd done just what I was supposed to do, and just to take deep breaths and know that everything was good, everything was going to be fine.

Meanwhile, he improved the stage set. He left Rufe Taggart where he fell, on his back, arms at his sides, as if waiting for someone to draw a chalk outline around him. The gun he'd meant to kill me with, the gun that had done me the kindness of jamming or misfiring, had skidded halfway across the room, and Vince bent over and reached for it, than thought better of it and used his foot instead. Years later I saw a little kid trying to dribble a soccer ball, and out of nowhere it reminded me of the way Vince gave the gun little nudges until he had it where he wanted it, maybe half a dozen inches from the dead man's outstretched right hand.

Like he never let go of it until he hit the floor, he said later. Not tampering with evidence, because the evidence was right there, telling anyone with eyes and a brain exactly what happened. But why leave room for confusion? You put the gun back where it should have wound up, you're just making an adjustment in the interest of clarity. You could even say you're doing what God would have done if he'd given the matter some thought.

I stayed where I was while he went off to check out the rest of the apartment, and when he didn't return right away I went looking for him. We needed to call it in, and I thought maybe he'd managed to find a working phone in an abandoned building, which was unlikely but not impossible.

What he found in the bedroom was two dead bodies, a woman and a boy. A mother, 27, and her ten-year-old son, and I can summon up their names but I can't see that anybody's life will be richer for my writing them down here. The medical examiner would find that she'd been killed first, strangled to death, possibly after having been rendered unconscious by blows to the head.

Taggart had kept the boy alive for quite a few hours, and found no end of ways to amuse himself. Somewhere along the way the kid died—and, everyone agreed, not a moment too soon.

All Vince and I knew at the time, in that back bedroom, was what we saw in front of us. I don't know how much of it I took in, or what I may have made of it; I was still hearing the echo of the shot I'd fired, standing there staring like a high school quarterback with a concussion.

He grabbed me, took me back to the first room, the one with only one dead body in it. He said, "You ever get a voice in your head, a pain in the ass voice saying how could you do that, how could you take a human life, just remember what you saw in there. What you did, on top of saving your life and mine, is you put down a fucking monster."

He looked hard at me, waiting to see if I was taking it in. I said, "That woman."

"The kid's mother. Gotta be."

"No," I said. "The woman who steered us here, the woman who called it in. She'll have a phone."

He looked at me. "Always thinking," he said. "How about if I just go out to the car and use the two-way?"

*   *   *

An exchange when he got back:

"You should be sitting down."

"No, I'm fine. What I couldn't figure out was the gun."

"What? You figured it out fine. You shot him before he could shoot either of us."

"He fired all those rounds. That's what the other woman heard, that's how come she called it in. But not at the mother and not at the kid, I went and checked."

"You went back in there?"

"There's shells all over the floor, same as in here. More than the gun holds, so at some point he reloaded. But no sign he shot either of them."

"So what the fuck was he shooting at?"

I pointed to a darkened corner to the left of the sink.

"Jesus, a rat?"

"Some people are afraid of them."

"He emptied his gun and reloaded? All to kill one rat?"

"He must have seen one in the bedroom, too, because there are empty shells on the floor."

"But no dead rat?"

"Not that I could see. Maybe there was just the one rat, and after he missed it in the bedroom he came in here after it."

"And killed it, finally, and made enough noise so we got the call." He took a closer look. "He really shot the shit out it, didn't he? I'm no fan of rats, especially in a house with kids in it, but your average rat's just trying to make a living, raise a family. Set traps, put out poison, fine, but I wouldn't want to open up on one with a tommy gun."

"He wasn't very good with a gun."

"And a good thing, too. Matt, lemme look at you. You're all right, aren't you?"

"I'm fine," I said.

* * *

And I was. Technically I suppose I was still in some sort of state of shock, but moving around the apartment had helped, and so did figuring out the reason for the gunshots. I had to look around and I had to think, and these were things a cop would do, so that's what I had to be, a police officer, not some gormless kid confronted with the consequences of his own hurried action.

Acting like a cop got me back to feeling like one. The guy was a threat, the guy was a monster, the guy was dead. Well, fuck him.

I was fine.

* * *

Things have changed. If you fire your weapon at anything out-side of the designated firing range, you can pretty much count on a couple of weeks of desk duty and a fairly elaborate inves-tigation. If you actually kill somebody, it gets amped up ac-cordingly, and psychiatric counseling is recommended, if not mandatory.

This was what, close to sixty years ago? They took my gun away long enough for ballistics to establish that it had been the source of the single round that exploded the left ventricle of Rufe Taggart's heart—and then they gave it back to me. They took my statement, oral and written, and went over it with me, and they asked me if I would be willing to see the shrink who got departmental referrals in cases like this, and I said I didn't really feel the need but I had no objections.

I kept my appointment. The shrink seemed ancient to me, though he was probably at least fifteen years younger than I am now. Wore owlish glasses, smoked a pipe. Diplomas on the walls, and an oil painting of a harlequin at a card table, playing solitaire.

Funny what sticks in your mind. Not his name, nor much of our conversation. At his request, I went over what had hap-pened at the crime scene, staying with the scenario as Vince and I had reported it—Taggart, aiming at me when I managed to shoot him first. I said a little about the state of shock I'd been in, like a kid who'd gotten his bell rung in a football game. I hadn't said much about that previously, and something in his expression encouraged me to add that I'd been puzzled about the gunshots, and how working it out that the guy had been shooting rats—or a rat, anyway—got me back to normal.

"Of course," he said. He asked about dreams, and if I was sleeping well, and if I'd found myself drinking more. I said if I'd had any dreams I didn't remember them, and I slept like a log. I said I generally had a beer when I got off duty, and sometimes two, and that hadn't changed, and he nodded, because that was what he wanted to hear. He probably got to hear it a lot, and most of us who spoke the words were lucky we weren't hooked up to a polygraph.

He told me I sounded fine, said a delayed reaction was always a possibility, and invited me to come in if there was ever a point where I wanted to discuss anything further. Then we got into sports, and he spent the rest of the hour telling me he still couldn't come to terms with the Dodgers having relocated to Los Angeles. "I still liked the players," he said. "Was it their fault O'Malley sold out the people of Brooklyn? Of course not. So I liked the players but I hated the team, and how is that possible?"

Food for thought.

A year or two later, after the promotion, and after my marriage had gone a little further downhill, there was a moment when I had the thought of going back for another session. It was a thought that came to me but not one that I chose to entertain, because what was the point? The best I could hope for was that it might help the man sort out his feelings about the Mets.

*   *   *

Shooting Rufe Taggart, shooting him dead, got me the gold shield.

There's no way to prove that. The promotion, when it came, did so in the wake of a collar Vince and I made in Dyker Heights. A Slope resident, the suspect in a string of burglaries, was in the wind, and he'd given a woman reason to wish him ill, and she found the card I'd given her and dialed the number.

Then she'd called him and told him what she'd done, and it was almost comic; the poor bastard was on his way out the door when we came along to knock on it. Any number of things could have happened, but all he did was say *Oh shit,* and managed to sound more relieved than dismayed. In the car he said, "You get tired, you know?" and that's all he said until his lawyer got there.

So it was a case that reflected well on us, but not the kind that gets headlines, or leads to promotions. But I'd done a good thing when I shot Rufe Taggart, that was something everybody could agree on, and perhaps more to the point I'd walked away from the whole business in an exemplary manner, and all of that must have earned me a spot on some unofficial short list.

Then we picked up our burglar in Dyker Heights, and that's all anybody mentioned when they made me a detective. Nobody ever said a word about Rufe Taggart.

*   *   *

It's funny. I haven't really thought about him in ages.

An odd process, writing all of this. This morning I started the day by reading what I'd written about him yesterday and the day before. The facts are all there, in as much detail as they need to be. Summoning up my own thoughts and feelings after all those years is not so much difficult as uncertain. I can tell myself what I thought and how I felt, but I find myself questioning the reliability of the narrator.

The most salient single fact, it seems to me, is that until we went into that abandoned building I had never pointed a gun at anyone, unless you want to count the water pistol I got for my seventh birthday. And before we left the premises I had shot a man, and killed him.

I'd fired at a man who had thrown down his gun. I could spend a lot of time trying to parse that. Was I simply following through on an action already in progress, pulling the trigger before I could take in the information that his hand was empty? Or did that fact register, if dimly, and did I then make a conscious or unconscious decision to gun down an unarmed man?

As noted, I was in shock afterward. I can't remember what thoughts may have been going through my mind, and couldn't trust them if I did.

Afterward, the more I found out about Taggart, who he was and what he'd done, the easier it was to brush all those questions aside. I don't suppose many people would have contended that the world was a poorer place for his having left it.

Every man's death diminishes me, John Donne wrote, *because I am involved with mankind.* And I get the point, it's not that elusive, but I can't say that I ever felt diminished by the death of Rufe Taggart, or guilty for having caused it.

*   *   *

Back to Taggart, who seems to have more of a grip on my mind now than he ever did back in the day.

"God doesn't make mistakes."

John Donne never said that, as far as I know, although I doubt he'd argue otherwise. It's a line I've heard many times over the years at AA meetings, and while it's tempting to dismiss the people who utter it as living proof of the statement's falsity, one does get the point.

If God *did* make mistakes, Rufe Taggart would seem to be one of them. It's easy enough to characterize him as pure evil, as I believe more than one person did in the press coverage of his death. (These were the same people who labeled me clean-cut, level-headed, and promising.)

Pure evil. I don't know what that is, or what it means. I know what a sociopath is, and God knows they aren't all that thin on the ground. They know what's good and evil, right and wrong, and don't feel this knowledge should prevent them from acting entirely in what they see as their self-interest.

Many of them wind up in prison. But others run corporations, or have successful careers in politics or the military.

I suppose, to come at it from another angle, they are all of them doing the best they can.

I suppose Taggart was doing the best he could. I suppose he had a childhood that combined with whatever was in his DNA to make him the hideous human being that he was. I suppose he was just playing out the hand he'd been dealt.

Well, so was I.

I want to get off this merry-go-round. I don't owe him anything. He got me my gold shield, but I'd have wound up a detective before too long anyway, with or without his help. He was trying to kill me, and would have done so if his gun had cooperated, and instead I killed him, and I never regretted it.

Not then and not now.

All these words, words I have to labor over, words I write and delete and write again, for a man whose chief distinction in this context is that he was the first person I ever killed.

And not the last.

*   *   *

I was excited about becoming a detective.

It meant a higher salary, of course, but that was the least of it. Far more important, it meant playing the game at a higher level, taking the cases that other patrolmen caught and really working them. It meant, too, the respect that came with that role, and not just the respect of others. I don't think I ever met an NYPD detective who wasn't proud to have earned that status.

It took me a few days to spot the downside. I wouldn't be working with Vince Mahaffey anymore.

I don't get it, I told him. Every hour I put in on the job I spent alongside him. It was the two of us in the room with Taggart, the two of us picking up the poor mope in Dyker Heights. It was always the two of us, Mahaffey and Scudder, Vince and Matt, first in our blue uniforms and then in our Robert Hall two-button suits, doing what we did and making a good job of it.

So why was I the only one getting the bump?

Because it was never in the cards, he said. Age alone was enough to rule him out, because when did they ever give a gold shield to a man who had more than half of his twenty in? But he could be any age and it didn't matter, because he wasn't detective material, and never had been. He didn't have the mind for it, he didn't have the education—

Education? Last I heard, we each of us had a high school diploma. Period.

—or the inclination, he said. He liked being a cop, it was all he'd ever wanted to be, and for all that was wrong with the job and the department, it was still where he wanted to put in his hours. He never had the slightest ambition beyond what he was, never thought about the sergeant's exam, never thought of the world beyond Brooklyn, or much beyond the bounds of the Seven-Eight.

I said something about turning down the promotion, staying where I was. They'd be moving me, a new rank generally meant a new precinct, and I'd been told to report to the Sixth Precinct on Charles Street in Greenwich Village. What did I know about the Village, for Christ's sake? All my snitches were in the Seven-Eight, my whole life as a cop was here, and who said I had to trade all that for a gold shield? They could have it back, I was happy where I was.

I don't know if I meant all that, but he was quick to shoot it down. I was meant to be a detective, he said, and he was not, and he'd miss working with me, but when all was said and done, each of us could get along without the other.

And so on.

I remember that conversation, in a bar he'd chosen in Carroll Gardens. You'd think it would have been an occasion that called for serious drinking, but two rounds was all either of us was up for. Outside, at a loss for something to say, I told him he was the best partner ever.

"We did each other some good," he said. "We had some good times. You okay to drive?"

I said I was, and he got into his car and I got into mine. I was indeed okay to drive, but the last thing I felt like was a long stretch behind the wheel with Anita at the other end of it. The hell with that.

I spent the night in my apartment, and spent much of it thinking about Vince. We'd assured each other we'd keep in touch, but I wondered how much I'd actually see of him, or he of me.

We'd stay friends, I thought, and then corrected myself, because how could we? We'd never been friends in the first place. We were partners, closer than friends in many respects, and there were things we talked about, things we told each other, but a partnership was not a friendship—although even now, all these years later, I don't know that I can explain the distinction.

Never mind. My marriage was circling the drain, my wife was probably having an affair, my kids were visibly growing up and invisibly growing away from me, and the relationship I was sitting up mourning was the on-the-job equivalent of a marriage of convenience.

* * *

Let's try this again.

I spent a couple of hours yesterday and close to an hour today writing about early days at the Six. About Eddie Koehler, who led the Detective Squad, and some of the other men I worked with. About how I was regarded with a certain amount of suspicion at first, and how that resolved itself, and a case or two that came to mind.

And I just now erased all of that.

I'd been told not to erase anything, that if I didn't like what I'd written I should just hit the return key twice and move on and write something else. Well, too bad. None of what I wrote yesterday or today is what I want to talk about.

All that needs saying, I think, is that I found my way into my new job without too much trouble. I liked some of my fellow detectives better than others, but I got along well enough with all of them without bonding all that tightly with any of them.

And I upgraded certain elements of my life. I wore my Robert Hall suits until Phil Aiello from Midtown North dragged me to Finchley's. I switched my answering machine for one that allowed me to call in and access my messages from a distance, and I set it up in a furnished apartment on West Twenty-fourth Street in Chelsea, a little nicer and way more convenient than Polhemus Place, and at a lower rent; I'd done a favor for the landlord, helped him unload a difficult tenant from another of his buildings, and the apartment was how he thanked me.

My new building was a brick rowhouse, four stories plus a basement. The first floor was half a flight of stairs above sidewalk level, the basement half a flight down; my apartment was in the basement, but it had a couple of windows, and a private entrance. And my name wasn't on the mailbox, or on a lease, all for a hundred a month, cash and off the books.

I got new business cards printed, but I managed to keep the same phone number. Somebody knew a guy whose brother-in-law was an installer for the phone company, and a few dollars changed hands, and from then on my Brooklyn phone number rang in a basement apartment on West Twenty-fourth Street, where my new machine waited to take a message.

I spent more nights there than I had on Polhemus. Sometimes alone, sometimes not.

*　　*　　*

I think there are moments when your life changes, and they may or may not seem consequential at the time.

An obvious one, I suppose, would be when I pulled the trigger and killed a man who'd just thrown down his gun. But where did the act take me that I wouldn't have gone otherwise? If we'd brought Rufe Taggart in alive, I'd have distinguished myself no less than I did by killing him, with that same gold shield just as surely in my future.

Was it one of those significant moments when I met Danny Boy Bell? If so, it's also a moment I can't recall with any certainty. I was already settled in at the Six when I got to know him, and I remember someone introducing us at Tony Canzoneri's, a natural place to get a drink after a fight at the Garden.

But I think we may have been introduced before, and certainly each of us already knew who the other was, and I have a feeling someone pointed him out to me when I was still in plainclothes at the Seven-Eight. It would have been in Manhattan, because I'd be surprised if Danny Boy ever got to Brooklyn, and it would have been at night, because otherwise he'd have been home with the shades drawn.

And he'd have stood out, wherever we were, because nobody

else ever looked like him. *Oh, that's Danny Boy, what everybody calls him, like the song. He's a professional snitch, but he'd probably call himself a broker of information. People tell him things, and word gets around.*

We got to know each other, and took to each other. He was a big fan of jazz, and knew a lot about it, and I'd found I was comfortable in the places where it was performed, and began paying more attention to what I heard there. And we both liked the fights, and one night we found ourselves ringside at the Garden. A welterweight named Vince Shomo was at the top of the prelim card, and a black man in an expensive suit was telling him something in a raspy voice. He looked familiar, and not in a fight crowd context. I couldn't make out what he was saying, but the fighter looked to be hanging on every word.

I don't know that the words of wisdom had anything to do with it, but Shomo knocked his opponent down twice in the second round and got a stoppage midway through the third, and the man in the suit was at his side as he headed for the dressing room. And paused to smile. "D-B," he said, in that voice. "Keep it close, my man."

"Always, Miles."

And Danny went on to tell me that was Miles Davis, which I'd managed to figure out myself by then, and that he'd heard Miles had an interest in Shomo.

And so on. If I had reason to seek him out, there were a couple of bars where I knew I was likely to find him. But most of our meetings were by chance, at one jazz club or another. We'd always exchange a few words, and sometimes he'd point to an empty chair and we'd listen to a set together.

Sometimes he'd have company. A girl or two, always attractive, white more often than not. I got the feeling they were mostly there as arm candy, though I'm not sure the term was around that long ago. (I could Google it, but it would be unsettling to find out Chaucer used it.)

And then there was a late spring night—June, I think, but it may have been around the end of May—when I found myself at loose ends. I was working two cases and both had stalled out, leaving me to await further developments. That's frustrating, you want to make something happen, but sometimes the only thing to do with your hands is sit on them.

Which made it a good time to head home to Syosset, but that was the last thing I wanted to do. I hadn't been home in a few days, and absence wasn't making the heart grow fonder.

I went to my apartment in Chelsea, and for the first time the place felt like a basement. I sat there and thought of people I could call and never got around to reaching for the phone.

I got out of there, hit a couple of bars. I walked out of one or two without ordering anything, and didn't have more than a single drink in any of the others. Everywhere I went was too loud or too quiet, too crowded or too empty, and I was harder to please than Goldilocks.

Then I walked into a jazz club on Hudson Street and my life changed.

*　　*　　*

The four musicians were in the middle of a set, and I found a seat at the bar and listened to them. A saxophone—an alto, I think—and a rhythm section. I'm not sure who any of them were, but if I had to come up with a name I'd say the horn player was Lou Donaldson. But that's more a guess than a memory.

I ordered a drink and drank some of it, and I looked around and it didn't take me long to spot Danny Boy. His table was close to the little stage, and he was sharing it with two women and an empty chair. While I was looking in their direction, Danny Boy said something and both women laughed.

Something made me want to be there, joining the conversation, maybe saying something that would draw laughter. Instead I stayed where I was, waiting for someone to return from the restroom and reclaim the empty chair. I wanted to be part of the party, but not in the capacity of a fifth wheel.

Looking back, it's hard to say why I was making all that much of it. A friend was at a table across the room from me, and what did it matter whether his party ran to three or four? Either way it was entirely appropriate for me to go over there, or at least catch his eye and acknowledge his presence.

Which I did, a few minutes later. One number ended, and the pianist announced the title of the tune with which they'd close their set. I got to my feet and moved to a more visible position, and when Danny Boy looked my way, I raised a hand. He did the same, and motioned me over, pointed to the empty chair. I took it, and all four of us gave the music our respectful attention.

When it ended, Danny Boy held up a hand for the waitress and made a circular motion to order another round. He introduced me—"This is Matthew, and he genuinely is one of New York's Finest"—and his two companions. The honey blonde was Connie, the dark-haired girl was Elaine. No last names for any of us, and no identifiers beyond the fact that I was a cop.

"Perfect timing," he said. "Matthew, they're taking twenty minutes, but the right mood-altering substances might lead them to stretch that to a half hour. Another set will be worth the wait, and your good company will make the minutes fly."

"Glad to help," I said.

I'd been able to tell from across the room that both women were attractive, and nicely dressed. That became even more evident at close range. We started talking, about the music at first, and then Danny Boy led us off on a tangent, and I couldn't tell you where it led, but it was probably interesting.

I held up my end of the conversation, encouraged by the fact that both women seemed fascinated by whatever it was I was saying. Our talk had what you might call a subtext, as each of us sized things up and made choices.

I'd liked the looks of both women, and Connie probably made the stronger initial impression, perhaps because she seemed to drink in everything I said. But that shifted. Elaine was paying a different kind of attention, and when I looked in her eyes I could see her mind working.

Ten minutes or so into the break, she got to her feet. "I need the little girls' room," she said, and glanced at Connie, who rose and joined her.

"Women always do that," I said to Danny Boy. "Whereas men—"

"Never do," he said. "I think it may have to do with sitting down to pee." He frowned. "Or not. In this instance, I suspect they're determining the direction the evening is going to take."

As indeed they were. When they came back Elaine said, "Danny, it's wonderful music, but I don't think I can handle another set. You won't hate me if I call it a night, will you?"

I asked if she was all right. She said she was fine, but her mind was all over the place, and it was probably the full moon.

She touched my hand. She said, "Matthew, could you put me in a cab? It's not that late, I could probably get one myself, but—"

I said of course I could and would, and I got to my feet and reached for my wallet, but Danny Boy signaled me to put it away. I said goodbye to him and to Connie and headed for the door with Elaine at my side, and halfway there she took my arm.

Outside, I said she wouldn't need a cab, I had my car and I'd be glad to give her a ride. She said her place was on East Fiftieth Street and was that too far out of my way?

I said that was exactly where I was going.

I'd parked at a hydrant on Spring Street, and I found an equally convenient hydrant on Fiftieth. I was an NYPD detective, by God, and I had a card I kept on the dashboard shelf that let me park anywhere in the five boroughs, with the possible exception of the Mayor's front lawn.

It was somehow clear, even before I offered to drive her, that we were going together to her apartment. Her doorman greeted her by name—"Good evening, Miz Mardell—" and we went upstairs to an apartment that was all black and white, and looked like something you'd see in a magazine.

She drew the door shut, turned the lock. We stood and looked at each other. It seems to me that her face showed a mix of emotions, dread among them, but that may be hindsight talking. I held out my arms, and she came into them, and we kissed.

*   *   *

Afterward, we talked. About a guy I'd taken into custody a day or two ago and the entirely unbelievable alibi he'd offered, and how it had turned out against all odds to be true. About a play she'd seen, which had been disappointing, and a wine-and-cheese opening at an art gallery downtown, which hadn't. That led me to mention the painting in her living room, a vivid abstract canvas, an explosion in scarlet.

She'd seen it a year ago, knew at a glance it was just what the room needed, knew too that she wouldn't get tired of looking at it. "And once it was on the wall I thought oh God, is this how it starts? Am I gonna be spending all my money on paintings? But nothing else ever grabbed me the same way. And I sort of like that it's the only thing in the apartment that's not black or white."

"Except for you," I said.

"Except for me. Oh, gee, Matthew. Or do people call you Matt? Danny Boy said Matthew."

Most people said Matt, I told her, but I liked hearing her say the full name.

"The intimacy of the formal," she said. And, testing the name, "Matthew." The silence stretched, until she laid a hand on my arm and said, "Oh, hell. I was afraid of this. I'm having a good time, Matthew."

"So am I."

"I'd like to see where it goes. I know it can't go anywhere, you're a married man, and I'm the last thing in the world you're looking for. And breaking up somebody's marriage is the last thing *I'm* looking for. Jesus, will you listen to me? You poor man, all you want to do is get your clothes on and get out of here."

I waited.

She said, "Otherwise there's a conversation we have to have, or how can we be on the same page? I mean, I know you're a policeman. But you don't know what I do. Or maybe you do."

"If I were to guess—"

"Yes, go ahead."

"Are you in the game?"

I'd heard her laugh lightly before, when I was telling her about the mope and his unlikely alibi, but now her laugh was rich and full-bodied. It made me want to amuse her so that I could get to hear it again.

"Oh, wow," she said. "I'm trying to come up with an opening sentence and you've already got the whole page. And you found the perfect way to ask. *Are you in the game?* If I'm not, I won't understand the question, so how can I take offense? What gave me away, Matthew?"

The intimacy of the formal. "Well, I'm a detective," I said.

"And your keen mind never stops working."

"When I went over to your table and got a close look at you and Connie, my first thought was you were models. Because you had the looks, and you were well turned out, and all."

"But then our innate whorishness came through."

"You could probably be a model. I'd say Connie's a little too full-figured for the fashion industry."

"She's got quite the rack, hasn't she?"

"Plus models always strike me as unsatisfied. Maybe it's because they're always worried that they're not attractive enough, or maybe it's just that they never get enough to eat."

"'And for lunch today I was a good girl. I had an apple and an enema.'"

"There you go. My next thought was show business. Actresses, possibly dancers, something like that."

"But?"

"But then Danny Boy asked me something, and I replied at some length, and I noticed the way the two of you were listening. Connie in particular was looking right into my eyes and hanging on every word."

"And what self-respecting actress would do that?"

"Except what I got was that she wasn't really listening. Oh, she was paying close attention, and if there was a test on the material she'd score high on it, but she was managing to look more interested in what I was saying than she really was. Her attention didn't go any deeper than her eyes."

"That's very interesting. What about me? Or were you only paying attention to Connie?"

"You were really listening," I said.

"Oh."

"Or you were a cut above her when it came to faking it."

"No, I was tuned in," she said. "From the moment you came over to our table. *Oh, he's a cop,* I thought, before anybody said a word, and—"

"You got that right away?"

"Instantly. Your eyes, your stance, your whole, what's the word, *affect*. I don't think you're cut out for undercover work."

"Just certain roles. I can get away with posing as a crooked cop."

That earned me that laugh again. She said, "So I saw this handsome cop, and I saw the ring on your finger, and I saw the look in your eye, and I knew."

"You knew?"

"That you'd be coming home with me. That if we were both genuinely lucky we'd do what we came here to do, and then you'd hop into your clothes and out of my life, and neither of us would ever be any more to the other than a happy memory."

"Is that what you want?"

"No," she said.

What she wanted, she said, might not be possible, and that might be true even if I wanted it as well. What she wanted was for us to go on being who we were, a happily married cop and a call girl who enjoyed her work, and for me to be her boyfriend. She didn't want me to take her away from all this, and she didn't want to take me away from anything, least of all my wife and children, but she'd like to have someone who mattered to her, someone to spend evenings like this with, someone to be close to both in and out of bed.

She hadn't had a boyfriend since her senior year in high school. He'd got her pregnant right around the time she began to realize he was sort of a yutz, and he would have married her, because that went along with being the kind of yutz he was, but thank God she said something to her Aunt Vicki, and Vicki had a cousin who knew somebody, and she had a quick and quiet abortion and that was that.

And two years later she was working in a Midtown office and one day she had lunch with a girl named Karen, who was showing off yet another cashmere sweater, and something made her ask Karen how she could dress the way she did on her salary.

"I go out on dates," Karen said. "I'm a very good date."

It took her a couple of seconds, but only a couple of seconds, and what shocked her was realizing that she wasn't shocked. She was interested, and not because she wanted to fill her drawers with cashmere sweaters. What she wanted was to get away from the house she'd grown up in, and a job she hated, and a future with nothing more interesting in it than a three-bedroom split-level in Levittown and a husband not much different from the yutz she'd come this close to marrying.

Karen introduced her to Rita, the woman who arranged her

dates, and two days later she got a call at work and told her boss she had a migraine. She could have walked the half dozen blocks to the hotel, but she told herself she was now one of those people who took taxis. "The Sherry-Netherland," she told the driver, and she didn't need to tell him where it was.

The john was wearing one of the white terrycloth robes the hotel provided. He'd just taken a shower, which she thought was considerate of him. He chatted with her for a few minutes, told her he was in town briefly from Indianapolis, that his unspecified business brought him to New York fairly regularly. He asked her if she would take off her clothes, and she did, and he told her she was very pretty. *I'll bet you say that to all the girls*, she thought, but she kept that thought to herself. Then he sat back and opened his robe, and it wasn't hard to figure out what he wanted her to do, and she did it.

She didn't have to collect payment. That would go directly to Rita, who'd pass along her share. When she'd gotten dressed, she gave him a warm smile and said she hoped she'd see him again sometime, and he told her she was sweet. "Something for yourself," he said, and slipped her what turned out to be a fifty-dollar bill.

She never looked back. As soon as she could afford it she moved into a studio apartment in Murray Hill, and by the time the one-year lease was up, she was ready for Fiftieth Street, where she'd been for close to three years now. She still got some of her dates through Rita, but most came as referrals from satisfied clients.

She'd never had a pimp. She knew girls who did, and they all came across to her as emotionally damaged, if in different ways. A number of them used drugs, which had even less appeal to her than giving her earnings to some uptown clown in a zoot suit and a purple hat. She'd gotten high on marijuana a couple of times, and tried cocaine, and none of that was for her. Nor was alcohol, really. She'd have a glass of wine, but rarely wanted a second.

So that's who she was, and that was probably more than I needed to know, but part of what she wanted was someone she could say anything to, and I felt like I might be that person, and if I wasn't then we might as well find that out sooner rather than later.

So what did I think?

I said, "Here's what I think. If I were wearing a white terrycloth robe, the kind they give you in fancy hotels—"

"Like the Sherry?"

"Kind of like that, yeah. And if I were to open it, what do you suppose it might get me?"

"A good time," she said. "I think we're both gonna have a good time."

*   *   *

We mostly did.

Once, twice a week. Usually at the black and white apartment in Turtle Bay, for as little as an hour or as long as overnight. I'd call, to make sure she was alone and would like company, and when I got there the doorman would confirm that Mr. Matthew was welcome.

Once in a while, she'd call me, and if she had to leave a message it would be to call my Cousin Frances. That happened infrequently enough that when she left that message some years later I'd forgotten the code, and it took a while before I figured out who'd left the message.

Sometimes when I'd call she'd have commitments. That was the word she'd use. Sometimes her machine would pick up, leaving me to wonder whether she was in the shower or getting her hair done or servicing some guy in the garment trade.

Or some lawyer. She got a lot of business from the legal profession.

And how did I feel about all that? I'm sure my feelings were mixed, and I'm at least as sure that I was largely out of touch with them. That's pretty much a given when you drink the way I did, and it's one of the reasons why they put the stuff in bottles.

Make the next one a double, Joe. I want to get out of touch with my feelings.

Hard to know, a lifetime later, just what I felt. There was some pride, certainly. There were all these men, richer and more successful than I, and they paid this woman for what she willingly gave to me. And she was beautiful, and whip-smart, and funny, and she chose to spend her time with me.

So I felt proud, and aware of my good fortune.

I also got to feel morally superior. No, not that, not exactly. More that I was able to feel on an equal moral footing.

Because, although I thought about it as infrequently as possible, I was not entirely at ease with the person I had become. I was watching my marriage fall apart. I was a poor father and a worse husband. I was drinking more than I should, and getting away with it, and trying not to acknowledge the possibility that there would come a day when I couldn't get away with it any longer. I was cutting corners on the job, and breaking the rules that a cop learned he could break, and a few others besides. I was getting away with that, too, but it was something to think about—or, with another drink in me, something to not think about.

But I was on the right side of the law, wasn't I? And if my morals were a little lax, well, why don't you take a good look at her? She broke the law every time she let a paying customer into her bedroom, and she earned a very decent living by leading a life that was anything but decent. For Christ's sake, she'd do things with strangers that plenty of women wouldn't do with their husbands. Hey, maybe you were less than perfect as a husband and a father and a cop, but still that's what you were, a husband and a father and a cop, and she was a whore.

Not a chain of thought that surfaced often, even as it's not one I like to recall. But it was there, and some of the time I took note of it, and had to blink it away.

And mostly we did have a good time, and mostly it felt less complicated than it was. We went to some clubs, heard some good music. We talked a lot, and I'm sure we told each other a few lies, but not too many.

I don't think I'd ever had a conversation with a woman where I hadn't been holding something in check, polishing the image I was presenting of myself. God knows that was true in my marriage. It worked, insofar as it worked at all, because I made myself appear to be the person Anita wanted me to be. With Elaine, I somehow knew I didn't need to do that. And the more I let her see into me, the more she seemed to like what she saw.

This morning I'm a little late getting to the computer. I woke up with something bothering me, and the first thing I did was take a book from the shelf and sit down with it. It's one of the novels, somewhere in the middle of the series, a rather dramatic thriller in which a lot of people get killed and—spoiler alert!—Elaine and I get back together again.

The novel includes a summation of how we met and got together in the first place, years before the story begins, and the facts are wrong. I join them at Danny Boy's table, but instead of a downtown jazz club the venue is Poogan's Pub, one of Danny Boy's regular hangouts. And there are other inconsistencies, which I guess I suspected, and that's what sent me looking for the book. Little things, mostly; she had one abstract painting on the living room wall, a splash of red in the black and white room, and in the book there are two paintings. Why make a change like that? One painting's not enough? It bothered me to read it, but I've had an hour or so to brood about it, and I'm able to see that it's not important.

The book, as I said, is a dramatic thriller, very much as the writer meant it to be. It begins with someone turning up from the past and changing the present and the future, and I suppose it does its job. The actual events in the book's present-time narrative are as I recall them, and I can't explain the other changes, but I guess he thought it would make the story more dramatic and more thrilling.

I never thought of it as thrilling while it was going on. I sure as hell wasn't getting a thrill out of it. It was dramatic, yes. I'd have been happy to have it a little less dramatic.

Never mind. If he could move my date of birth from September to May, I suppose he's as entitled to shift our meeting site from SoHo to the West Seventies.

*   *   *

Back to early times—which happened to be the brand of bourbon Elaine kept for me. It was nothing special, Early Times, but it didn't have to be. It went down easy, and did the job.

We did each other good, and in ways beyond sex and conversation. Once or twice, maybe more than that, she'd been able to recount something she'd heard from a john that wound up making a case for me. She never had to testify or give a statement, and if I cited her at all it was as an anonymous source, but she set some processes in motion, and one of the cases generated a headline or two.

And what did I do for her? Well, it's often useful for anyone with a marginal lifestyle to have a good friend with a badge. When a doorman told her a police officer had asked him some questions, I managed to identify the cop in question and have a talk with him. She's all right, I said. She's a valued source, and a close personal friend. Say no more, he told me, and that was the end of that.

And one time one of the things every working girl dreads happened to her. A john had a heart attack or stroked out, whatever it was, and died in her bed.

Since then I've seen a T-shirt that said, *A friend will help you move. A real friend will help you move a body.* I got an urgent message to call Cousin Frances, and that gave me the chance to prove I was a real friend.

That's in the novel. And it's letter-perfect there, too, down to the street in the Financial District where I dropped the corpse, and the $500 I took from his wallet, and shared with the patrolman who gave me a hand. I figured the dead man would want me to have it, for sparing his wife the knowledge that he'd taken his last breath in a prostitute's bed.

So we played a variety of roles in each other's lives. And, when a real threat came along, I was the one who figured out a way to deal with it.

That was probably something that I could have handled better.

*　　*　　*

It's all in the book, accurately enough and in detail, and the last thing I want to do is relive it all here. But it was pivotal, and a summary seems to be called for.

A man named James Leo Motley, a sadistic psychopath out of a nightmare, decided to move into her life—and the lives of a few other women, Connie Cooperman among them. I got Elaine to file a complaint, but there was no real way that was going to stop him, and the best thing I could do was set a trap for him.

It worked, but not as well as I'd hoped. We wound up in hand-to-hand combat, and I don't know that I'd have come out of it well if he hadn't turned out to have a glass jaw; my elbow found it, and that was all it took.

He'd entered her apartment illegally, of course, and on an earlier visit he'd committed a brutal anal rape, and he'd hurt her on more than one occasion with his unaccountably powerful fingers. There was a whole list of offenses he'd committed and laws he'd broken, and there was no way they added up to a case that any District Attorney would rush to prosecute. She was a whore, for God's sake, and I was a cop who spent a lot of time with her, and even the greenest Legal Aid lawyer could make me and Motley look like two rival pimps. Or he'd offer to plead it out, and the DA would congratulate himself for sticking the son of a bitch with ninety days in Rikers.

What I wanted to do, of course, was kill him, break his neck and dump him somewhere. But it was one thing to relocate a corpse after a heart attack and another to do the same for a murder victim. And, while I had in fact shot a man dead without being greatly trouble by the act, that had happened in what I guess you could call the heat of battle, and in the course of performing my duties as a police officer. With Motley I'd be killing a man who wasn't even conscious. There was no way it could be anything but murder.

So, having remembered the man I shot, I remembered too how Vince Mahaffey had improved the optics of the crime scene, moving the cast-aside pistol so that it was where it would have been had its owner been holding it when he fell. I frisked Motley, and was pleased to find a gun; I wrapped his hand around it and used one of his powerful fingers to pull the trigger, firing a couple of rounds into the living room wall. (And didn't miss the painting by much.)

Then we figured out our testimony, but in the end nobody had to testify, or undergo cross-examination. I made my report, and Elaine and Connie gave statements, and a charge of attempted murder of a police officer got plea-bargained down to aggravated assault, and Motley stood up in court and drew the agreed-upon sentence of one-to-ten in Attica.

I wish to God I'd killed him when I had the chance.

*　　*　　*

What we'd gone through with Motley was the sort of thing that would either bring two people closer together or push them apart. In our case, I think it probably did a little of both.

We had been in a dangerous situation together, and had come through it unharmed as a result of our joint efforts. In the course of so doing, we had perjured ourselves and falsified evidence and put a man in prison—not an innocent man, it would be hard to find a less innocent man, but nevertheless a man who had not done what we'd sworn he'd done.

I'd perjured myself before. I won't go so far as to call it part of the job description, but it's a rare police detective who's spent much time in the witness chair without tailoring the facts to fit the requirements of the case. Exactly what you saw, precisely what you heard—well, you were there, and you know what happened, and there's no question the sonofabitch did what he's accused of, so why leave a two-inch gap that some prick of a defense attorney can drive a tank through?

Nor did Elaine's line of work entail a reverence for truth. If she did her work well, every man who left her bed did so convinced she'd enjoyed their time together, that she'd found his conversation fascinating and his lovemaking thrilling. Many of her clients were in fact interesting men, and every now and then she'd actually allow herself to go with the flow and genuinely treat herself to the orgasm she'd otherwise feign—but that was only once in a while.

Our sort of shared experience dissolves barriers. I've sometimes thought it was like a presence—an elephant in the room, if you like—visible only to the two of us. It gave us something to talk about, but it was always there, whether we wanted to talk about it or think about it or not.

One immediate effect was that we found ourselves with a need to keep our relationship hidden. Now I'd been a married man all along, so it's not as though we'd run around town looking to get our names in the tabloids, but we'd been comfortable enough in a restaurant or a jazz club. Now we saw each other only in her apartment, and those visits were infrequent until Motley was on his way to Attica. And, even in a cell, he cast enough of a shadow to keep us conscious of a need for discretion.

*   *   *

Something I haven't thought of in years, and maybe it's pertinent. One weekday evening, maybe six months after the resolution of the court case, we'd moved from the bedroom to the living room. She'd fixed me a cup of coffee and flavored it with a shot of Early Times, and had popped the top on a can of Tab, and said casually that she'd be leaving in a few days for a week on a yacht in the Caribbean.

Whose yacht?

"Some rich guy," she said. "He's celebrating something—grinding the faces of the poor, most likely, so he invited three friends and told them to bring somebody."

"And you're somebody?"

"This one fellow was a client, but I checked my book and it squares with my memory, which is that I only saw him three times and the last time was a year and a half ago."

"I guess you made an impression."

"I think he thinks I'm classy enough to use the right fork at meals and not embarrass him. He almost said as much. My guess is we won't spend a lot of time making Martian cars."

That was shorthand. There was a joke she'd told me, a couple of Martians visit Earth, and one of the things they want to know is how human beings reproduce. A verbal description doesn't really work, so two scientists volunteer to have sex while the visitors observe the process. And halfway through the Martians start giggling, and wind up laughing uproariously. What was so funny? "On Mars, that's how we make automobiles!"

"Well," I said. "I hope the weather's good."

"Just so I don't get seasick. I don't usually, but I did once, and it's something you never forget. Oh, you know what you should do? While I'm gone?"

"Cry myself to sleep?"

"Call Connie."

"Connie?"

"Connie Cooperman. She'd love it if you called."

"Seriously?"

"Absolutely. She thinks you're cute. You could have had her the night we met, if I hadn't called dibs first."

"And you wouldn't mind?"

"I'll be two thousand miles away throwing up over the side of the boat, and you're gonna be with somebody, and why wouldn't I want it to be somebody decent?"

I never did call Connie. I looked up her number once, and was on the point of dialing it when my phone rang and a snitch had something for me that couldn't wait. And one night when I might have called her was spent taking my boys to a college basketball game in Hempstead. Hofstra was playing somebody, maybe Adelphi, and I forget why we went. I think somebody must have given me tickets.

And, you know, the week went quickly enough. Then she was back, and we were as we'd been, though something was a little bit different. I wasn't sure how I felt about her steering me in her best friend's direction. It was at once a generous act, showing that she cared for what she saw as my best interests, and at the same time clear evidence that she wouldn't mind if I slept with another woman, even with someone close to her.

*   *   *

I can't seem to work out just how long it was between the time James Leo Motley headed upstate to Attica and the incident in Washington Heights that led me to end my career as an employee of the City of New York. I could probably contrive to look it up, the events at both ends of the interval are matters of public record and not hard to access. In all likelihood, I could manage it in a matter of minutes, and without leaving my desk.

But I don't seem to feel like looking that long and hard at that part of my life. It was probably more than a year and less than two, and in the course of those months, however many of them there were, I went on doing what I did while every aspect of my life deteriorated.

I wouldn't have been able to tell you as much. I realized, at least some of the time, that things were not going well. I was getting less satisfaction out of my work, and two men at the Sixth Precinct, one a desk sergeant and the other a fellow detective, had somehow taken up residence on the list of people with whom I no longer got along. I did my work, and the only notes added to my file were the occasional commendation, but my heart was not always in it, and it was hard to summon up the energy required to put in the extra hours.

This was a new development, I'd always been the eager beaver, turning to off-the-clock work as an alternative to heading home to Syosset. If I noticed the difference, I told myself it was natural; the novelty of the gold shield had worn off, and it had become just a job. If I managed to do my job, well, that was plenty.

I viewed both my relationships in much the same way. I was providing for my family, my wife and kids weren't missing any meals, and if I wasn't around much, well, how many marriages were a bed of roses? We argued more, Anita and I, and long silences marked much of our time together, but we managed to present a united front to the kids, and now and then we'd go out to dinner, and once in a while we'd find ourselves in bed together and remember that there were things one could do in a bed besides sleep.

One night, when an extra drink or two had led to just that, I lay at her side afterward with the conviction that we'd each of us had someone else in mind throughout. I almost said as much, but she was already asleep, and moments later so was I.

With Elaine, arguments weren't a factor, or long silences. But I found myself calling less frequently, and when I did call she was a little less receptive. And the time we did spend together, in or out of bed, was less than it had been.

As I said, with Motley awaiting trial we'd quit going out in public, and we never picked it up again. No dinners in quiet French or Italian restaurants, no nights catching Monk at the Five Spot or Chet Baker at Mikell's.

We still had sex, when I went over to her apartment, but our conversations before and after were truncated, and somehow less intimate.

And, to the extent I took notice, I guess I saw this as inevitable. An affair, I'd have said, was not altogether unlike a marriage; in each, time played an erosive role, and sooner or later washed away the best elements.

And what did I do with the time I wasn't devoting to being a cop or a husband or a boyfriend?

Well, I was spending a lot of it on West Twenty-fourth Street. I'd taken it so I'd have a place to sleep when I didn't go home to Syosset, and I spent a lot of nights there. (I'd also had it in mind as a place to bring women, and in the several years I had the place, I'd used it all of two times for that purpose.)

Now, though, I wasn't just sleeping there. I'd go there when I didn't have any place else to go, and I'd find some music on the radio, and open a bottle, and pour a drink, and when the glass was empty I'd pour another.

I knew that solitary drinking was cause for concern if not alarm, but I also knew it had certain advantage. It was, God knows, a cost-effective alternative to drinking in bars. It spared you the company of people you'd just as soon not sit next to, let alone talk with. And, if you drank as much as you wanted, the process of getting home and to bed could be tricky. If you'd driven to wherever you were drinking, you had the choice of driving home drunk or, the following day, trying to remember where you'd left your car.

In your own apartment, you could tune the radio to the station of your choice instead of trying not to listen to what some clown played on the jukebox. And when you'd had the evening's last drink, the one that cuts the brain in sections, you didn't have to worry about getting home. You were already there.

*   *   *

All right, fast forward.

There came an evening I've gone on about often enough in the past. For years it found its way into my qualification every time I told my story at an AA meeting, and it's recounted in some detail in all of the early novels, to the point where I have to believe people got tired of reading about it.

(I said as much to LB. He said it was valuable information, it supplied motivation. I suggested it was time to start leaving it out, and since then he's mostly done so. And he confessed that in one book he has me report that I fired uphill at the robbers, and in another that they were downhill from me when I fired at them, and that two unrelated readers actually spotted this discrepancy and wrote letters pointing it out to him. Just for the record, he wondered, was it uphill or downhill? I said I didn't remember.)

So, briefly: One evening I finished a tour of duty, the last two hours of which I essentially stole from the city; I was still on the clock, but I'd stopped working a case and went to Twenty-fourth Street, where I ate a sandwich from the bodega on the corner and found a beer in the fridge. Then I took a nap, and when I woke up around eight-thirty I thought about driving to Syosset.

I'd fallen asleep with the radio on, and while I was thinking about the drive they broke for a weather report, and rain was in the forecast. It never did rain that night, in the city or out on the island, but they told me it was likely to, and that made my decision for me. I didn't want to drive clear to Syosset in a downpour, or even in a drizzle.

I wish I hadn't heard the forecast. I wish I'd decided the hell with it, I could drive in the rain, I was a big boy, I wouldn't melt and neither would my car.

I decided I wanted a drink, and I looked to see if there was a bottle in the apartment, but there wasn't. There rarely was, those days, because an open bottle quickly became an empty bottle. There was a liquor store around the corner, and I could get there and back in ten minutes. I'd decided to do just that, to pick up a fifth of Early Times or Ancient Age or some other lower-shelf bourbon and settle in to listen to some music. Easy enough, I already had the radio on . . .

That's not what I did, although I've always wished it were.

I'm dragging this out and can't think why. I decided I didn't want another night of solitary drinking, not just then. And I thought of Elaine, not for the first time, and picked up the phone and dialed her number, and got a busy signal. I could have waited five minutes and tried again, but instead I copped a quick resentment, because why did she always have to be talking to somebody else when I was trying to reach her?

I left the apartment, I got in my car. I was driving with no destination in mind, and then I remembered a place someone had dragged me to once, way the hell uptown in Washington Heights. It was a pleasant place to spend an hour or so, it was never packed and never empty, the guy behind the stick poured a good drink, and if the jukebox ran a little more to country and western than I might have preferred, it went okay with bourbon. The only question was whether I could find the joint.

I could, and did. The bartender remembered me, and even remembered what I drank.

*　　*　　*

And what do I remember, really?

When something runs in your mind for years on end, when you've recounted it endlessly to yourself and to others, what are you actually recalling? The event itself? Or memories of the event, reflected infinitely in an unending series of mirrors?

Haven't I been over this enough?

*　　*　　*

One more time, then.

I didn't see them come in. I was at a table, I'd paid for my drink at the bar and walked over to a table where a captain's chair promised a more comfortable seat than the backless bar stool. I should have seen them come in, because I was a cop, and in that capacity I was charged with being fully aware of any room I was in—of who was in it with me, and who left, and who entered. It didn't matter that I was off-duty. Just as I was still required to be armed, so I was still supposed to use my eyes and ears.

But I wasn't paying attention, not to them when they entered or to much of anything else. I suppose I was listening to whatever was playing on the jukebox, although I wasn't paying any real attention to that, either. Then the bartender was saying, "Okay, okay," and I looked in his direction, and I saw him facing two men with their backs to me. He was handing them something—money from the cash register, it would have been—and my mind began to register what I was seeing, the way the men were standing, a shaft of light glinting on what would have been a gun.

Gunshots, and people crying out, and by the time I was on my feet and my gun was out of its holster the shooters were out the door. I went after them, and we were all of us outside on the street, and they ran uphill or downhill, whichever way it was, and what difference could it possibly make?

Did one of them turn and fire at me? I sometimes think so, but can't be sure it ever happened. It might be something I'd prefer to believe in order to justify what happened next. But whether or not it happened is about as important as the upward or downward slope of the street.

I dropped to a knee. I cupped my right elbow in my left hand—this was before they began teaching the two-handed grip—and I saw that I had a clear shot, and I fired, and kept firing until the gun was empty, as I'd been taught early on.

It was good shooting, you'd have to call it that. I hit both of them, killing one outright and essentially crippling the other. And it was a righteous shooting; they'd shot the bartender dead, as it turned out, and they had guns in their hands when I shot them, and there was a woman on the scene to report that they'd been shooting at me, although that kind of eyewitness testimony is ultimately no more persuasive than my own uncertain memory.

And if that were all there was to it, I'd have been a hero cop, a man who was in the right place at the right time and did the right thing, and my life would have gone on. It would have fallen apart sooner or later, because that was the overall path I was on, but that might have taken a while. The mills of God do what they do, like it or not, but they do it in their own sweet time.

But that wasn't all there was to it, because my revolver held six rounds, and while four of them hit the men I'd aimed at, two did not. And one of those errant bullets bounced off something, the pavement or a stone stoop, some damned thing. Something that redirected it without slowing it down as much as one might have hoped, and it hit a little girl in the eye and went on through into her brain and killed her.

Instantly, they said.

Her name was Estrellita Rivera. Estrellita means Little Star. I don't know what Rivera means, and neither does Google Translate. I don't know what she was doing out on the street at that hour, either, but she had more right to be there than I had to shoot her.

* * *

As far as the world was concerned—the NYPD, the press, the man on the street—I came out of it okay. The men I shot had violent criminal records, and the bartender was probably not the first person to die at their hands.

Nobody had thought to check my blood alcohol, but I'd

probably have been all right if they did. I'd bought just one drink at the bar and left it unfinished when I ran out after them. As for what I was doing in a neighborhood ginmill some eight or nine miles north of my own neighborhood, well, I was a police detective known for pursuing leads and cultivating sources on my own time. Wasn't that explanation enough?

I got the benefit of the doubt. Cops generally did, and I'd say they still do, more often than not. Though more so in some neighborhoods than others.

*   *   *

There was no trial. One of the men I'd shot had died at the scene, which was his Get Out Of Jail Free card. The other, when he got out of the hospital, told everyone that his partner had gunned down the bartender—although ballistics evidence indicated otherwise. It didn't really matter, the DA charged him with two counts of felony murder, and let him plead to a lesser charge that still put him away for twenty-to-life.

Still, all of this took some time. I turned in my gun, of course, and went on leave, and there was a stretch of a couple of months when nothing happened.

Other than drinking, which I did a lot of. I was at home in Syosset for a while, until I drove into the city and burrowed into my apartment in Chelsea. At first I left it only to walk to and from the liquor store, but liquor stores get held up all the time, just ask my Uncle Norman, and I got fixated on the notion that somebody would hold it up while I was buying my bottle of bourbon, and what would I do now that I didn't have a gun?

No problem. They were more than happy to deliver, and I never had to leave my apartment.

Of course I did leave, eventually. By the time I was done I'd left everything—the job, the family. All of it.

*　　*　　*

Yesterday I spent the whole morning at my desk and didn't write a word, just sorting out the stretch from settling in on Twenty-fourth Street and checking in thirty-three blocks uptown. I couldn't get a handle on it, it was like trying to get a handhold on a column of cigarette smoke.

Here's how it might go in a movie: We see a man sitting on a sofa, drinking. Then cut to the same scene, but he's gone three days since his last shave, and a side table that was empty before now was two empty bottles on it. Then the same scene again, but now there are four empties on the table, and one more on the floor at his feet.

Then a montage: the entrance of a police station. A desk, onto which a hand tosses a gold shield. A man leaving the room, light glinting on the shield he's left behind.

And whatever else. In a car, driving eastbound on the Long Island Expressway. The same car, parked in the driveway of a modest suburban home, and the man emerges from the house with a suitcase in each hand, and walks on past the car and on down the sidewalk.

Maybe we see him on a platform, with a train pulling into the station. Then walking through Penn Station, still carrying those suitcases. Or we skip all that and just show him getting out a taxi in front of the Hotel Northwestern. The suitcases are at his feet as he signs the registration card. They're in his hands as he exits the little elevator and walks the length of a threadbare hall carpet to the room he's just rented.

He unlocks the door, brings the bags inside, puts them down, closes the door and engages the lock. It's a small room, minimally furnished, and he walks to the single window and we see the imposing apartment building on the south side of Fifty-seventh Street and, some miles in the distance, the new twin towers of the World Trade Center.

There's a table next to the bed, with a phone on it. He sits on the edge of the bed, reaches for the phone, but we get the sense that he can't think of anybody to call.

*   *   *

—*You weren't supposed to let me read this. 'Don't show it to anybody, not even Elaine.'*

—*I'd say it depends who's doing the supposing. My own supposition is that I'm the one who's writing this, and I get to decide who reads it. How on earth could I write about you and not show you what I'd written? You read the whole thing?*

—*No, duh, just the sentences with my name in them. Of course I read the whole thing.*

—*It's pretty much all stuff you already knew. But I thought . . .*

—*Excuse me, but like hell it is. How come you never told me you had a brother?*

—*I don't have a brother. Where did you get that from?*

—*Where indeed, and just who are you gaslighting here? All these years, and I never knew a thing about Joseph Jeremiah Scudder, and . . .*

—Oh, Jesus. You said I never told you I had a brother, and I got this image of a living brother my own age, and I never had one, and it didn't occur to me that you meant . . .

—Your baby brother.

—I never mentioned him?

—Never.

—Are you sure?

—I'd remember. One of the first things I ever told you about myself was I was an only child, and you said so were you. And more than once over the years we've commented on the fact that neither of us ever had any brothers or sisters, and now that we've both reached the age where everybody starts forgetting everything, you suddenly remember your brother Joe.

—I never think of him.

—You never think of him? Honey, you sit down to write about your life and you mention him on the first page.

—I guess something triggered it. Looking back at those first years, which is something I don't do often. I swear I never decided not to tell you about him, because the thought never came up. Look, didn't you say that your parents tried to have more children?

—Yes, and they might have, if they could have figured out a way to accomplish it without touching each other.

—Didn't you tell me your mother had a miscarriage?

—That was before I was born. I never got the details, I don't know what month she was in, but I don't think she was very far along. She lost the baby, and then two years later she got pregnant again, and that turned out to be me. And she never got pregnant again, although the implication was that they forced themselves to try.

—*And you mentioned it to me, but only in passing, because it wasn't that big a deal to you.*

—*Well, why should it be? The baby she lost, if they even knew what it was, a boy or a girl, I can tell you nobody bothered to mention it to me. Your brother was born and lived a few days and had a name and everything.*

—*All I can say is I never think of him. I never saw him, I never knew him, and he never had a chance to make much of an impression.*

—*And your mother was never the same, and your father was never the same, and if you think none of this had any impact upon little Mattie . . .*

—*Maybe. Huh.*

—*What?*

—*'Don't show it to anybody, not even Elaine.' I'm beginning to think the sonofabitch knew what he was talking about.*

*   *   *

—*You really think Anita was having an affair?*

—*I got that impression. There was this couple lived down the block from us.*

—*In Syosset?*

—*Uh-huh. We were over there once on a Sunday, he liked to put on an apron and grill hotdogs. Except they weren't hotdogs, he was from Wisconsin and the sausages had a special name. Bratwurst, that's what he called them. 'Come on over for some beer and brats.' At first I thought he was talking about his kids.*

—*And you think Anita took a liking to his bratwurst?*

—*You had to say that, didn't you?*

—*Pretty much, yeah. Seriously, what did you do? Use your magical cop intuition?*

—She spoke admiringly of him, and said it was a shame his
wife let herself go the way she did. And then she stopped
talking about him, and that struck me.

—The dog that didn't bark in the nighttime?

—Something like that, but I shrugged it off. What I told
myself was that I'd only had the thought because I wanted
it to be true.

—Why would you want . . .Oh, sauce for the goose?

—Maybe. If she's got something on the side, I don't have
to feel guilty about how I'm living my life. But I didn't
really dwell on it, and then we were going through a bad
patch . . .

—You and Anita.

—. . . and she more or less said she was seeing somebody. I
don't remember how she put it, but the implication was
clear. I could have picked up on it, and I think that's what
she wanted me to do.

—But you didn't.

—No. She must have known I got the message loud and
clear, but I didn't do anything with it, and it never came
up again. I suppose I thought about it from time to time,
and there must have been moments when I entertained the
wistful fantasy of the two of them running off together, but
I don't think there was ever much chance of that. You can
take the girl out of St. Athanasius, etc.

—Who was he, do you happen to know? Not Herr Bratwurst,
Saint Whatchamacallit.

—Athanasius. No idea. So yes, I'm reasonably certain she had
an affair, although I don't think it was the kind that would
put Antony and Cleopatra in the shade. But whatever
it was, it was over half a century ago, and so was our
marriage, and the woman's been dead for twenty years.

206 • Lawrence Block

—*Can it really be that long?*

—*I think it's more like twenty-two, and don't ask me where the time goes. When I went to her funeral, that must have been the first time in ages that I thought about her adventure with the bratwurst guy.*

—*You thought about it at her funeral?*

—*You think about everything at funerals. That's why people go to them.*

*   *   *

—*Lee Konitz.*

—*What about him?*

—*The alto player the night we met. It wasn't Lou Donaldson, it was Lee Konitz.*

—*I'll take your word for it.*

—*And the club was the Half Note.*

—*Of blessed memory. Didn't I say as much?*

—*You just said Hudson Street.*

—*Whatever. You're sure it wasn't Lou Donaldson?*

—*Positive. It was Lee Konitz.*

—*Who died a couple of years ago, if I remember correctly, though whether he died before or after Lou Donaldson I'd be hard-pressed to say.*

—*Lou Donaldson's still alive. He'll be 96 on the first of November, and it's only been a couple of years since he retired. Don't look at me like that. You really think you're the only one who knows about Google?*

*   *   *

—*I never saw that apartment. I knew you had a place but I don't think I knew where it was. On West Twenty-fourth Street?*

—*Just west of Ninth Avenue.*

—*But you thought you'd be better off in a hotel?*

—*I don't know what I thought, and I'm not sure you could call it thinking. I'd have something running around in my mind, and I'd go act on it. The idea came to me, and the next thing I knew I was down at Charles Street, putting in my papers and handing in my shield.*

—*Your famous gold shield. You threw it down on the desk.*

—*No, that's how they'd show it in the movie that thank God we'll never get to see. I handed it to Eddie and he handed it back and we did that little dance, like two guys on Forty-seventh Street who keep selling each other the same diamond, and eventually I walked out of there without it. I didn't turn in my gun because they already had it.*

—*Since the . . .*

—*Since the shooting, right. I never did go back on duty, so I never saw the gun again.*

—*I'm glad of that. The idea of you holed up with a bottle and a gun . . .*

—*I don't remember any suicidal ideation. A lot of things crossed my mind around then, but eating a gun wasn't one of them.*

—*Even so. When a man's having a breakdown, and . . .*

—*Is that what I was having?*

—*I don't know if they'd call it that now. A mental health episode?*

—*Whatever. The most self-destructive thing I did, besides*

flooding my liver with more alcohol than it knew what to do with, was give my keys back to my landlord. Who gives away a rent-controlled apartment?

∗ ∗ ∗

It's hard to understand why I gave the keys back to the landlord. I owed a few months' rent by then, but he wasn't pressing me, and I could have written a check for it readily enough. Then, when I finally made the break with Anita, I wouldn't have had to look for a hotel room.

That would have been the way to go, if I'd known what I was doing or where I was going. But I'd come to know I was done being a cop before I realized that I was also done being a husband and father, and giving up the apartment was of a piece with giving back my badge and gun.

Twenty-fourth Street had been a part of the job, an invaluable accessory as long as I was working out of the station house on Charles Street. But I was done there. I was going to be living full-time in Syosset, and what did I need with a crash pad in Chelsea?

It took less than a month in Syosset for me to see that being a cop wasn't the only part of my life that had run its course. There was a moment, while I was packing my two suitcases, that I thought of calling my landlord and finding out if he'd installed another tenant yet.

I didn't make the call. Part of it, I suppose, was a reluctance to feel like more of an idiot than usual, but along with that I had the sense that my circumstances called for a new start in a new part of town.

My hotel room cost more than I'd been paying on Twenty-fourth Street, and provided me with considerably less than half the square footage. Instead of a private entrance, it came with an attended desk I had to walk past every time I came in or went out. Now and then I'd think about the apartment I'd given up, and wish I hadn't—but not often, and not with any real regret. I'd made the right move.

* * *

And I made the right move letting Elaine read what I've written, although it's cost me a few days at the computer. There was no reason to say anything to her about the project, not early on, but as the words mounted up it began to feel as though I was withholding something from her, something increasingly substantial as one day's work followed another's.

We talked at length about what I'd written—I've reproduced a portion of it here—and then she broke off in the middle of a sentence and said that was enough. "I don't want to get in the way of what you're doing," she said.

* * *

So here I am, back at it.

One thing she'd commented on was my first partner, Vince Mahaffey. She'd never met him, of course, but he'd figured in a lot of the stories I told. She wanted to know whatever became of him, and if we'd stayed in touch.

Of course we'd said we would. And of course we didn't, not really. I switched station houses, from the Slope to the Village, and in the process I'd left Vince behind with my silver shield and my Robert Hall suits. Not consciously, not intentionally, but that's what happened—and it was in the nature of things for it to happen.

We were never friends. We were closer than friends, in many respects, but what bonded us was not the pleasure we took in one another's company as much as the role we played in our lives on the job. We were partners, joined together in an enterprise that always threatened to be perilous, its perils by no means limited to the ever-present possibility that someone could start shooting at us. Either of us could at any moment be called upon to save the other's life, and that's a stronger bond than generally exists between two fellows who live on the same block and get together every Saturday for eighteen holes of golf.

I can recall only two meetings and a phone call after our partnership ended. The phone call was first, and when I placed it I must have been a month or so into my time at the Sixth. I was in Syosset, the boys were asleep, Anita was at a friend's house, and I turned off the television set and picked up the phone. He sounded surprised to hear from me, and a little guarded at first, as if something I knew was now about to come back and bite him.

But it didn't take long before the edge went away. He updated me on some guys we both knew at the Seven-Eight, and I found something to say about whatever case I was working at the time, and we wished each other the best. And that was that.

I was glad I'd called, but realized I was unlikely to dial that number again.

Then an early case we'd had finally came up for trial, and both of us were called to testify. We each had separate briefings with an ADA, then both showed up at the courthouse on Schermer-horn Street. I was in a suit—I was always in a suit—and I was surprised to see Vince in his blue uniform.

He was called first, and he'd barely gotten past stating his name and rank when the two opposing lawyers paused for a sidebar. Next thing anybody knew, they'd arranged a plea deal and the judge was dismissing the jury.

Outside, I asked him if he had time for a drink. "Right around the corner," he said, "if you don't mind drinking in a room full of lawyers."

The place he took me to was dark and quiet, and we bought drinks at the bar and took them to a table. I observed that he'd reversed the usual order of things; back before we moved up to plainclothes, we'd always show up for court dates in suits, and today he'd left the suits in the closet and put on his old uniform for the court appearance.

"But I guess it worked," I said, "because all you had to do was state your name and swear to tell the truth and nothing but the truth, and that scared the sonofabitch into copping a plea."

He laughed, and picked up his drink, then put it down and said, "No, see, this is what I wear all the time these days."

"They put you back in uniform?"

"At my request. My insistence, I should say, because the first thing they did was tell me what I wanted was irregular."

"Irregular?"

"'Highly irregular, Officer Mahaffey.' Hey, why do I want to spend good money on suits? Plus it's simpler this way. You put on the blue bag, you don't have to figure out which tie goes with it."

"Okay."

He laughed. "That's a polite way of saying I must be crazy, but not really. Moving up to plainclothes was a great opportunity, and one I've got you to thank for—"

"Oh, come on."

"No, it's true, and we both know it's true. And I started wearing suits and I got the job done, so I could have stayed where I was after you made it across the bridge. And in fact I did, and they partnered me up with a guy named Alfie Riordan, I don't know if you knew him—"

"I don't think so."

"—but he was okay, we got along all right, but what I realized was I missed the uniform. I hadn't known I missed it when it was you and me, but now I did. I like walking down the street, or just sitting over a cup of coffee, and everybody who looks at me knows they're looking at a cop."

"You think a suit changes that?"

"I guess I've got the look. All these years, but to tell you the truth I think I always looked the part. School I went to, there was always someone looking to steer you toward the priesthood, but with me they didn't bother. They looked at me and knew where I'd wind up."

"Destiny," I said.

"Something like that. But kids, little kids, they only know you're a cop when they see the uniform." His face darkened. "Some of 'em, they get to be a certain age, you're something to be afraid of. But the rest, and especially the younger ones, what they see is someone who's there to protect them. That's what they see, and it shows on their faces." He shrugged. "And, you know. I guess I like that."

Afterward I wasn't sure how to feel. The return to uniform felt like a step backward, a regression, but he seemed happier for it. I remember thinking that he was more content being what he'd always been than I was with my well-cut suits and my gold shield, but I didn't spend a lot of time thinking along those lines.

Truth to tell, I didn't think often of my old partner.

The next time he showed up was from a distance—in the paper, and on the local news. There was one of those investigations into police corruption that come up every few years, this one centered on Brooklyn, with the Seven-Eight one of four or five precincts in the spotlight. They'd set up a commission to investigate, headed up by a hungry young ADA fresh out of St. John's law school, and you'd recognize his name; the publicity he stirred up ultimately got him all the way to the Governor's Mansion in Albany, and he might have stayed there longer if he'd been able to keep his pants buttoned.

The scandal that returned him to private life felt a lot like poetic justice, but it didn't have anything to do with Vince Mahaffey, however satisfying he may have found it. Vince came under fire for two missteps—taking money from a probable drug dealer and giving false testimony in a criminal trial.

He did what you do, he cooperated with the commission but not with enthusiasm, dragging his feet and implicating his fellow officers as little as possible. In return, they let him retire. He had his twenty in, and five or more years on top of that, and he got to put in his papers and collect his pension.

But they took the badge and the gun, and he couldn't wear his blue uniform anymore.

While this was going on, I paid it as little attention as possible. I didn't think I had anything to worry about myself, although I'd cut enough corners during my time at the Seven-Eight. I'd taken money, of course, and on occasion I'd stood up in court and sworn to tell the truth only to put a spin on it. But all of that was history, and it was Brooklyn history at that, and I was in Manhattan and I didn't figure it would touch me. And it didn't.

I thought about reaching out to Vince, and I didn't, and I've regretted it on occasion, although it never kept me up at night. There were good reasons not to reach out, as any contact I initiated might prompt some eager beaver to take a look at me, and even if it didn't go anywhere it would be attention I'd rather avoid.

And what could I say, or do? What good would it do either of us?

*　　*　　*

I did see the man one more time.

It was a year or two after my move to the Northwestern, and I'd long since settled into what seemed to be my new career as an unlicensed and essentially unprofessional private detective. I'd think of myself and sometimes describe myself as doing favors for friends, but not everybody who hired me was in any sense a friend, and I got paid for the favors I did. It was, I guess, a way to go on being a cop, and a way to go on eating and drinking and having a roof over my head. I couldn't think of anything that might suit me better, and still can't.

Sometimes the favors I did sent me out of Manhattan, and not infrequently to Brooklyn. A few of those ventures wound up in books; one that didn't sent me back to Park Slope, and actually led me to the site of my first apartment, on Garfield Place. That gave me a turn, and something made me check out Polhemus Place while I was in the neighborhood, and there I was, remembering moods and incidents that hadn't crossed my mind in ages.

Then I got back to business, and with a little effort I found my way to the Chemical Bank branch on Ovington Avenue, where I was hoping to get some information out of an assistant manager. I went through the revolving door and walked some ten or twenty steps past the uniformed guard when something registered sufficiently to make me turn and look at him, and it was Vince Mahaffey.

For a moment I thought he'd managed to get reinstated, because the uniform he was wearing wasn't that different from the one he'd worn on the job. But the cut was different, and the color was softer than NYPD blue, and the badge on his chest was a rent-a-cop special that could have come out of a box of Captain Crunch.

But it was definitely Vince. He looked older, and he'd put on a few pounds, and something else—he looked somehow diminished, as if this paler uniform made him a less forceful man.

I stood there looking at him, and I was still enough of a cop that it didn't occur to me to try not to stare. Maybe he felt my gaze, maybe he was just accustomed to scanning the room, but he turned toward me and I saw recognition come into his eyes. He said my name and I went over and we shook hands.

He said, "Jesus, Mattie, I hope you're not here to hold us up. All the time I been here I never once had to put my hand on my gun, let alone draw it."

I told him what I was there for, and who I'd be seeing.

"Oh, him," he said. "Guy's a pussy. He'll tell you anything you want to know, and if you push him he'll give you the keys to the vault. Let me look at you. You look okay."

"So do you, Vince."

"I read about you a few years back. That was a righteous shooting, up in Washington Heights, but it must have given you grief."

We talked some about that, just skimming the surface, and he said I must have heard or read about his troubles, and I acknowledged that I had. He said the PBA's lawyer had been all you could ask for, and he'd come out of it with his pension and health insurance, and if he'd wanted to he could have gone straight to Florida.

"I could have afforded it," he said, "though just barely, and every morning the big decision would be the beach or the golf course, but either way that's more sun than my Irish skin's happy with. So every morning I come here instead, and I point customers in the right direction and stare down the ones who look like they don't belong here, and maybe once a month some drunk or nut job comes in and I take him by the arm and escort him outside."

I said it sounded okay.

"It's fine," he said. "It's not the most interesting work in the world, but how interesting does a job have to be? The time passes, and it's hard to believe, but before you know it I'll be collecting two pensions and getting two checks every month. And you know what? I still won't go to Florida."

"And meanwhile," I said, "you get to wear the uniform."

He nodded, and was silent for a moment. Then he said, "You know, when I was a kid, I never said to myself I wanna be a bank guard when I grow up. If there's ever been anyone who did, I never heard about it. But kids, the young ones, they come in here holding their mother's hand, their father's hand, you know what they see? They see a cop."

My turn to nod.

"So yeah, Mattie, I get to wear a uniform. And it's not the genuine article, and there's no question it's a comedown, but it's not so bad. It's really not so bad."

That was the last time I ever saw him. I don't know if he got his twenty years in, but if he did manage to qualify for a second pension he stayed in Brooklyn, because he was sitting quietly with a shot and a beer in a Park Slope tavern when he slumped to one side. The bartender knew CPR, remarkably enough, but he was gone and there was no bringing him back.

His was a funeral I'd have gone to, but it came and went weeks before I got news of his death.

Elaine was right. She wondered what had become of Vince, as anyone reading this might wonder. So it's as well I spent a couple of days remembering it and getting it written down.

But I can't say I found much joy in it.

*   *   *

Have I completed this assignment, such as it is? Have I written enough?

I wonder. I've covered, in as much detail as seems appropriate, the first thirty-five years of my life, from the cradle to what looked to be my professional grave. I've had a second life since then, and perhaps a third, and half a century has passed, but it seems to me that there's already a sufficient printed record of those more recent years.

It runs to a whole shelf of books, something like seventeen novels and another volume's worth of shorter stories. They have Lawrence Block's name on the cover, but they have mine as protagonist and narrator, and they're told in LB's approximation of my voice. They are properly described as works of fiction, with the understanding that fiction does not imply lack of truth so much as a willingness to refashion factuality in the service of drama, and perhaps in search of a higher truth.

That last sentence has the ring of blather, but I'll let it stand. I can't think of a better way to say what I mean.

A whole shelf of books, as I've said, and I can't see the point now in repeating their contents here, stringing one after another to tell my life story. I don't want to do that, and I'm even less inclined to pick those books apart, whining that this one had the time sequence twisted and that one has me working two cases at once, while in fact they took place several months apart.

I'll let the books stand. And, you know, I've read them all, and most of them more than once. Memory is a shape-shifter, and by now the novels and stories are as much a part of what I remember as the actual original events.

But for all the years I lived across the street at the Northwestern, the drinking years and the sober years, surely there were interesting things that happened, personally and professionally, that never found their way into print. Wouldn't some of them make interesting reading, even as they filled in the picture of how I spent those years?

Well, perhaps. Episodes come to mind, one involving an Armstrong's regular I haven't thought of in years, but when I think of summoning up the memories and fitting words to them, all I feel is an abiding weariness.

*　　*　　*

But I keep thinking about Motley.

James Leo Motley, of whom I've already written; it was he who tried to move in on Elaine's life, and whom I very deliberately framed for a variety of charges, including the attempted murder of a police officer. I falsified evidence, I prepared to offer up perjured testimony in court, and I'd have done so with an untroubled conscience but for the plea agreement that aborted his trial. He went off to prison, and it would be hard to argue that there was a more appropriate place for him anywhere above ground, and I didn't feel anything but satisfaction in watching him led off in handcuffs.

What I felt was triumph. I'd been painstaking and resourceful, and I'd made good use of the skills I'd learned on the job, and I'd solved a problem.

Just like that.

And it certainly didn't keep me up nights. It wasn't something to think about when I was looking into a glass of bourbon for an answer that wasn't there, nor did I ever feel the need to talk about it at an AA meeting. When I did the program's fourth and fifth steps, essentially reviewing my life and coming to terms with the parts of it that disturbed me, I don't think JLM even came to mind. If I ever thought of him, he'd have been in the column of matters I'd handled successfully and well, and so I could feel free to forget him.

As if.

Motley, I have to say, spent a dozen years doing everything he could to stay forgotten. He served more time than his maximum sentence, the extra years earned by bad behavior. He contrived to kill two or three of his fellow prisoners during his confinement, his guilt manifest if unprovable. He certainly stood a good chance of dying within the stone walls, of natural or unnatural causes, but he survived, and eventually he got out.

Sustained, perhaps, by a single-minded passion for revenge.

Because, in his mind, I had cheated. I hadn't played the game fairly. I was a police officer, sworn not merely to uphold the law but to obey it, and instead I'd fabricated evidence and brought charges against him that I knew to be false.

That's not fair! That's a cry that rings out over the years on every school playground, because if there's one thing every child seems to be born knowing, it's that life is supposed to be fair.

And, if there's one lesson he learns sooner or later, it's that it's not.

The last thing Motley said, before they took him out of that courtroom, was that he and I had unfinished business, that he'd settle up with me and all my women. Most men on their way to prison keep their mouths shut, but not a few offer up a threat on their way out the door, and maybe it makes them feel better. Cops and judges and officers of the court, the recipients of those threats, learn early on not to take them seriously.

Still, you notice. And what resonated with me at the time was not any actual danger his words might represent but the nagging thought that the sonofabitch wasn't altogether wrong.

Oh, make no mistake. Even if you waste a moment with the observation that he, like everybody else in this and any other narrative, was doing the best he could, that doesn't change the fact that he was a very bad man on his way to the place he truly belonged.

But he was right. I had not played fair, I had broken the rules, I had violated my own sworn oath. I had in fact employed unlawful and unethical and—yes—an unfair means to bring about what I believed to be a desirable end, an end I thought justified that means.

Well, you got me there, I could have said. *You're right, I broke the rules, I didn't play fair. And you know what? Fuck you.*

Well, it's all there in the novel. He served his time, his full sentence and then some, and walked out of there with just one thing on his mind. I won't say that thoughts of revenge kept him going through all those years, I can't know that, but he never ceased to entertain them.

And he didn't waste time acting on them, either. He started with Connie Cooperman, Elaine's best friend, who'd managed the very rare but not unheard-of feat of falling in love with a john, a decent man who was at once sophisticated enough to embrace her and her past and innocent enough in his heart to love her. He took her to a town in Ohio, and married her, and had three children with her, and the five of them were somewhere in the middle of Happily Ever After when Motley tracked them down and butchered the lot of them.

The details don't matter, not here, not now. Motley literally added insult to injury, so arranging the scene that the Massillon police concluded from the jump that local businessman Philip Sturdevant had for unfathomable reasons murdered his wife and children before taking his own life.

Horrible, certainly, but clear-cut, and an easy case to close. And while they were wrapping it up and signing off on it, Motley was cutting a story out of the newspaper, addressing an envelope to Elaine, and heading for New York.

Where he killed a lot of people, the bastard. He'd have killed me, he had his chances, but he was saving me for last. He very nearly killed Elaine.

"She has a good heart," the surgeon told me, when it was clear she was going to live.

No kidding.

And, at the end, if there's ever an end to anything, I tracked him down to the apartment where he was holing up. He'd gained access by killing the lawful occupant, because why not, but I found him, and the same glass jaw that had betrayed him years earlier on East Fiftieth Street let me knock him out.

LB wanted to change that in the novel, said it was all a little too Achilles-heel for his taste. I said that was what happened, which ought to count for something, and how could you write about Achilles and forget to mention his heel?

I remember that apartment, though I couldn't tell you the neighborhood, let alone the address. Not now, though it may very well come to me. But what I remember more than anything else is the mean musky stench of the place. It stank like an animal's lair, some foul-breathed predator's with a stash of half-gnawed bones in one corner.

I don't know how long I sat there, breathing that air, cradling his unconscious form. I'd once again put a gun in his hand, but I didn't fire shots into the wall. Instead I put the muzzle of the gun in his mouth and laid my fingers on top of his. And I waited, knowing what I had to do and somehow unable to get it done.

Until he began to stir, and I did what I had to do.

And do I regret so doing? No, and why on earth should I? I wasn't even cheating, not this time. I was playing fair. The rules of the game had changed, they were Kill Or Be Killed, and it wasn't a difficult choice to make.

If I regret anything, it was the action I'd taken years earlier in Elaine's apartment. I regret what I did—the false evidence, the perjured testimony—not because of the unfair means but of their long-term end. When I'd staged that scene, I'd started a process that would lead to the deaths of five people in Ohio and several more in New York. How could I fail to regret all that?

Here's what I wish I'd done. I wish I'd set the scene, firing those shots into the wall, and then I wish I'd drawn my gun, my service revolver, and put a single bullet where it would do the most good. His head, his heart. Whatever.

I've lived a long life, and in its course I've killed some people. One was an innocent child, and I could hardly fail to regret that, but it was never anything but accidental, and the scars it left me with have faded over the years.

I can't say the others bother me. Perhaps their failure to do so points to a defect in my character. I don't suppose it's for me to say.

But I've apparently reserved my deepest regret for a sin of omission, an instance where I might have killed but didn't. I think of the lives that might have been spared, the harm that might have been averted. Why, for the love of God, didn't I kill James Leo Motley the first time I had the chance?

* * *

And yet.

After the shooting in Washington Heights, it was years before I saw Elaine again. When I'd moved out of my life and into a room at the Hotel Northwestern, I did speak with her a couple of times, in connection with one case or another. Our phone conversations were cordial, but brief and to the point, and neither of us ever suggested we get together for a drink or a meal.

Then Motley turned up, and Elaine's immediate response was to call me, and we were flung violently together.

And we've been together ever since.

I think it surprised us both about equally, not just that we wound up in bed together but that each of us had been unwittingly waiting for us to find our way back to one another. Her life had changed less than mine, she was still in the same apartment and still engaged in what the world had not yet come to call sex work, while I'd been on an extended odyssey to a quasi-career as a private detective in sobriety. The people we'd initially been had fallen in love without having the wit to realize it; the people our lives had made us were at least bright enough to cling to each other until our eyes were open and we could see what was going on.

It doesn't really need to be talked about here, nor do the words come all that easily. But the point is that I can't say with conviction that all of this would have happened without the unwelcome intervention of James Leo Motley. I might contend that our bond was too strong not to reassert itself sooner or later, that we were destined for one another irrespective of circumstances, and perhaps that's true, but when I think the thought I can't block out the line Hemingway wrote for Jake Barnes:

> *"Isn't it pretty to think so?"*

One of the promises of AA is that we will not regret the past nor wish to shut the door on it. My own view is that nobody who pays attention to his life can be entirely free of regret, but there's another way to look at it, and that's that anyone genuinely happy with the present has to be grateful for every turn in the road that got him here.

My life, even as I see it drawing to a close, is richer and more gratifying than anything I could have thought to hope for. I never expected to live this long, or to find myself so content.

There are aspects that are less than perfect. I've lost people to death, and have drifted away from others. I rarely see Michael, my elder son, and for all the warmth I feel for him and his wife and my grandchildren, I find myself with little to say to any of them.

I can't even remember when I last heard from his brother. I have no idea where Andy might be, he never seems to stay in one place for very long, and the existence of another Andrew Scudder, who's evidently achieved some prominence in Mixed Martial Arts, makes a Google search for my Andy unavailing. For a while he stayed in loose touch with Mike, but then he stopped calling, perhaps embarrassed by how much money he owed his brother.

I'm pretty sure drink and drugs play a significant role in his story, so there's always the chance he'll find his way to the same answer I found, in one form or another. A lot of people do, but most people don't, and I'll type the words I've been avoiding: For all I know, he's already dead and buried. I hope otherwise but it's certainly possible.

I may never know.

There was a homeless black kid, around fourteen when I met him, who became a virtual son to me and to Elaine. Watching him grow, watching his life take shape, was a distinctly parental pleasure. When I was sufficiently committed to life at the Parc Vendôme to give up my hotel room across the street, I got him settled in there. He had come to serve as my assistant, revealing a natural talent for whatever it is that a private detective does, and as I found my way into retirement, he got acquainted with the stock market and discovered an uncanny aptitude for day-trading. That didn't take too big a bite out of his day, and he spent the rest of his time unofficially auditing college classes at Columbia.

In the novels, as in life, I knew him only as TJ. He was a constant presence in our lives, and then a frequent presence, one that could only become less frequent as time did what time does. He's now, astonishingly, a middle-aged man, with a house in Westchester County and his-and-hers SUVs in the garage, and his oldest daughter is the age he was when he and I first encountered one another in Times Square.

We see him and his wife every now and then. But we don't really know her at all, and barely know TJ. We know the boy he was and the young man he was becoming far better than we know the man he is today. So we see him infrequently, and that seems to be often enough.

On Friday evenings I go, more often than not, to my AA meeting in the basement of St. Paul's. Some years ago I was taken aback to realize that I'd been sober longer than anyone else in the room with me. Nowadays that's almost always the case. The meetings engage me less than they did early on, but I never leave one wishing I'd stayed home. And if I dozed off during one of the longer shares, well, it's an article of faith that the meetings work just as well if you sleep through them.

And Elaine has a program of her own, composed of working girls who'd left the life—or were trying to leave it. It's had a few names in the handful of years it's been functioning—the most recent was Sex Workers in Recovery—but they're still finding their way. Elaine was a long time out of the game when she found the group, but it's been therapeutic for her even as it's allowed her to be a sponsor and mentor. And she's found friends there.

And who else do we see? Well, Mick and Kristin. They're certainly our closest friends, and sometimes it seems as though they're our only friends. The bond is an uncommonly strong one, and Elaine has suggested that one element of it may be that the Ballous are the only couple we know who are as unlikely as we are.

McGuinness and McCarty . . .

Regrets? Yes, of course. There are things I could have done better. But no bitter regrets, not really, because I truly like where I am.

And the trip that got me here has had its moments.

MY NEWSLETTER: I get out an email newsletter at unpredictable intervals, but rarely more often than every other week. I'll be happy to add you to the distribution list. A blank email to lawbloc@gmail.com with "newsletter" in the subject line will get you on the list, and a click of the "Unsubscribe" link will get you off it, should you ultimately decide you're happier without it.

LAWRENCE BLOCK is a Mystery Writers of America Grand Master. His work over the past half century has earned him multiple Edgar Allan Poe and Shamus awards, the U.K. Diamond Dagger for lifetime achievement, and recognition in Germany, France, Taiwan, and Japan. His latest novels are *Dead Girl Blues* and *The Burglar Who Met Fredric Brown*; other recent fiction includes *A Time to Scatter Stones*, *Keller's Fedora*, and *The Burglar in Short Order*. In addition to novels and short fiction, he has written episodic television (*Tilt!*) and the Wong Kar-wai film, *My Blueberry Nights*.

While some Bernie Rhodenbarr fans might argue the point, Block's novels and short fiction featuring Matthew Scudder are generally regarded as his finest work. Beginning with *The Sins of the Fathers,* we follow the ex-NYPD detective for half a century; we watch him grow and age in real time, we see his alcoholism become increasingly problematic until the day when he leaves a drink untouched on the bar. (Two of the novels have been filmed— *Eight Million Ways to Die* and, more successfully, *A Walk Among the Tombstones*.) Finally, in *The Autobiography of Matthew Scudder,* we get see the man in full, from his boyhood in the Bronx to the twilit present.

Block contributed a fiction column to Writer's Digest for fourteen years, and has published several books for writers, including the classic *Telling Lies for Fun & Profit* and the updated and expanded *Writing the Novel from Plot to Print to Pixel*; he recently held the position of writer-in-residence at South Carolina's Newberry College. His nonfiction has been collected in *The Crime of Our Lives* (about mystery fiction) and *Hunting Buffalo with Bent Nails* (about everything else), while his collection of columns about stamp collecting, *Generally Speaking*, has found a substantial audience throughout and far beyond the philatelic community. He is a modest and humble fellow, although you would never guess as much from this biographical note.

Email: lawbloc@gmail.com
Twitter: @LawrenceBlock
Facebook: lawrence.block
Website: lawrenceblock.com

CPSIA information can be obtained
at www.ICGtesting.com
Printed in the USA
BVHW042021080623
665645BV00003B/24

9 781954 762213